HERGÉ
★
THE ADVENTURES OF
TINTIN
★

RED RACKHAM'S
TREASURE

EGMONT

The TINTIN books are published in the following languages:

Alsacien	CASTERMAN
Basque	ELKAR
Bengali	ANANDA
Bernese	EMMENTALER DRUCK
Breton	AN HERE
Catalan	CASTERMAN
Chinese	CASTERMAN/CHINA CHILDREN PUBLISHING
Corsican	CASTERMAN
Danish	CARLSEN
Dutch	CASTERMAN
English	EGMONT UK LTD/LITTLE, BROWN & CO.
Esperanto	ESPERANTIX/CASTERMAN
Finnish	OTAVA
French	CASTERMAN
Gallo	RUE DES SCRIBES
Gaumais	CASTERMAN
German	CARLSEN
Greek	CASTERMAN
Hebrew	MIZRAHI
Indonesian	INDIRA
Italian	CASTERMAN
Japanese	FUKUINKAN
Korean	CASTERMAN/SOL
Latin	ELI/CASTERMAN
Luxembourgeois	IMPRIMERIE SAINT-PAUL
Norwegian	EGMONT
Picard	CASTERMAN
Polish	CASTERMAN/MOTOPOL
Portuguese	CASTERMAN
Provençal	CASTERMAN
Romanche	LIGIA ROMONTSCHA
Russian	CASTERMAN
Serbo-Croatian	DECJE NOVINE
Spanish	CASTERMAN
Swedish	CARLSEN
Thai	CASTERMAN
Tibetan	CASTERMAN
Turkish	YAPI KREDI YAYINLARI

TRANSLATED BY
LESLIE LONSDALE-COOPER AND MICHAEL TURNER

EGMONT
We bring stories to life

Artwork copyright © 1945 by Editions Casterman, Paris and Tournai.
Copyright © renewed 1973 by Casterman.
Text copyright © 1962 by Egmont UK Limited.
First published in Great Britain in 1959 by Methuen Children's Books.
This edition published in 2002 by Egmont UK Limited,
239 Kensington High Street, London W8 6SA.

Library of Congress Catalogue Card Numbers Afor 813 and R 558597
ISBN 978 1 4052 0623 5

Printed in China
9 10

RED RACKHAM'S
TREASURE

THE ANCHOR
BAR
'Morning.
BAR
Ahoy there! . . . Bill! . . .
WHITE
Hello, George! How's yourself? . . .
Not so bad. And you? Still a ship's cook?
Still the same. I'm sailing aboard the SIRIUS in a few days, with Captain Haddock and Tintin. Know them?
Tintin? . . . Captain Haddock? . . . I certainly do. There's been plenty of talk about them - over that business of the Bird brothers.* But the SIRIUS - she's a trawler, isn't she? Are you going fishing? . . .
Yes, but it's not ordinary fish we're after, it's treasure!
What's that you say?
Well, it's like this . . . There's a treasure that belonged to a pirate, Red Rackham, who was killed long ago by Sir Francis Haddock aboard a ship called the UNICORN. Tintin and Captain Haddock found some old parchments . . .
. . . written by Sir Francis . . . who escaped from the ship . . . They know just where the UNICORN sank and . . . I'll tell you the rest later. These walls have ears.

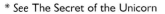

* See The Secret of the Unicorn

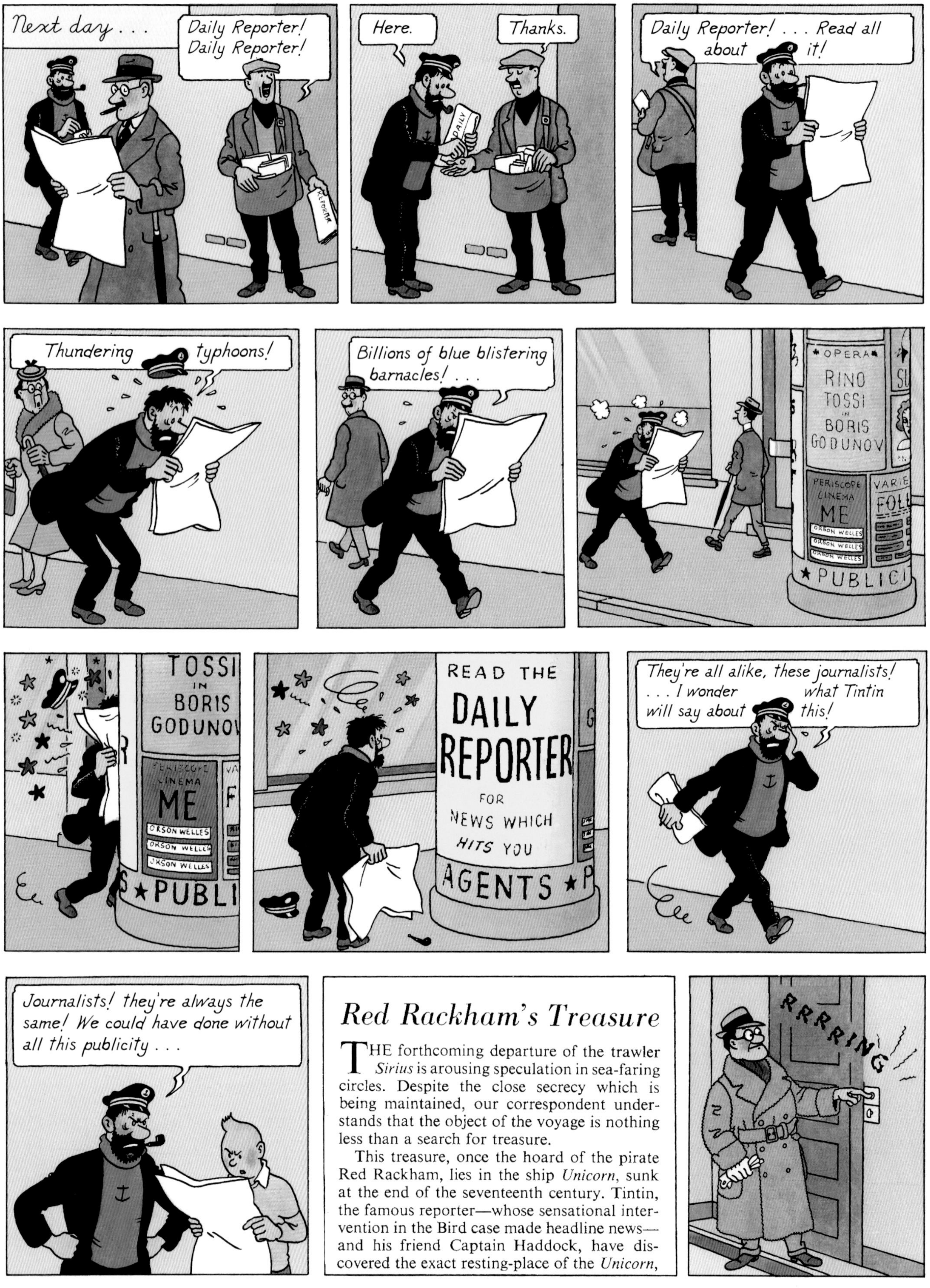
Next day . . .
Daily Reporter! Daily Reporter!
Here.
Thanks.
DAILY
Daily Reporter! . . . Read all about it!
Thundering typhoons!
Billions of blue blistering barnacles! . . .
OPERA
RINO TOSSI IN BORIS GODUNOV
PERISCOPE CINEMA
ME
ORSON WELLES
PUBLICI
TOSSI IN BORIS GODUNOV
READ THE DAILY REPORTER FOR NEWS WHICH HITS YOU
AGENTS
They're all alike, these journalists! . . . I wonder what Tintin will say about this!
Journalists! they're always the same! We could have done without all this publicity . . .
Red Rackham's Treasure
THE forthcoming departure of the trawler Sirius is arousing speculation in sea-faring circles. Despite the close secrecy which is being maintained, our correspondent understands that the object of the voyage is nothing less than a search for treasure.
This treasure, once the hoard of the pirate Red Rackham, lies in the ship Unicorn, sunk at the end of the seventeenth century. Tintin, the famous reporter—whose sensational intervention in the Bird case made headline news—and his friend Captain Haddock, have discovered the exact resting-place of the Unicorn,
RRRRING

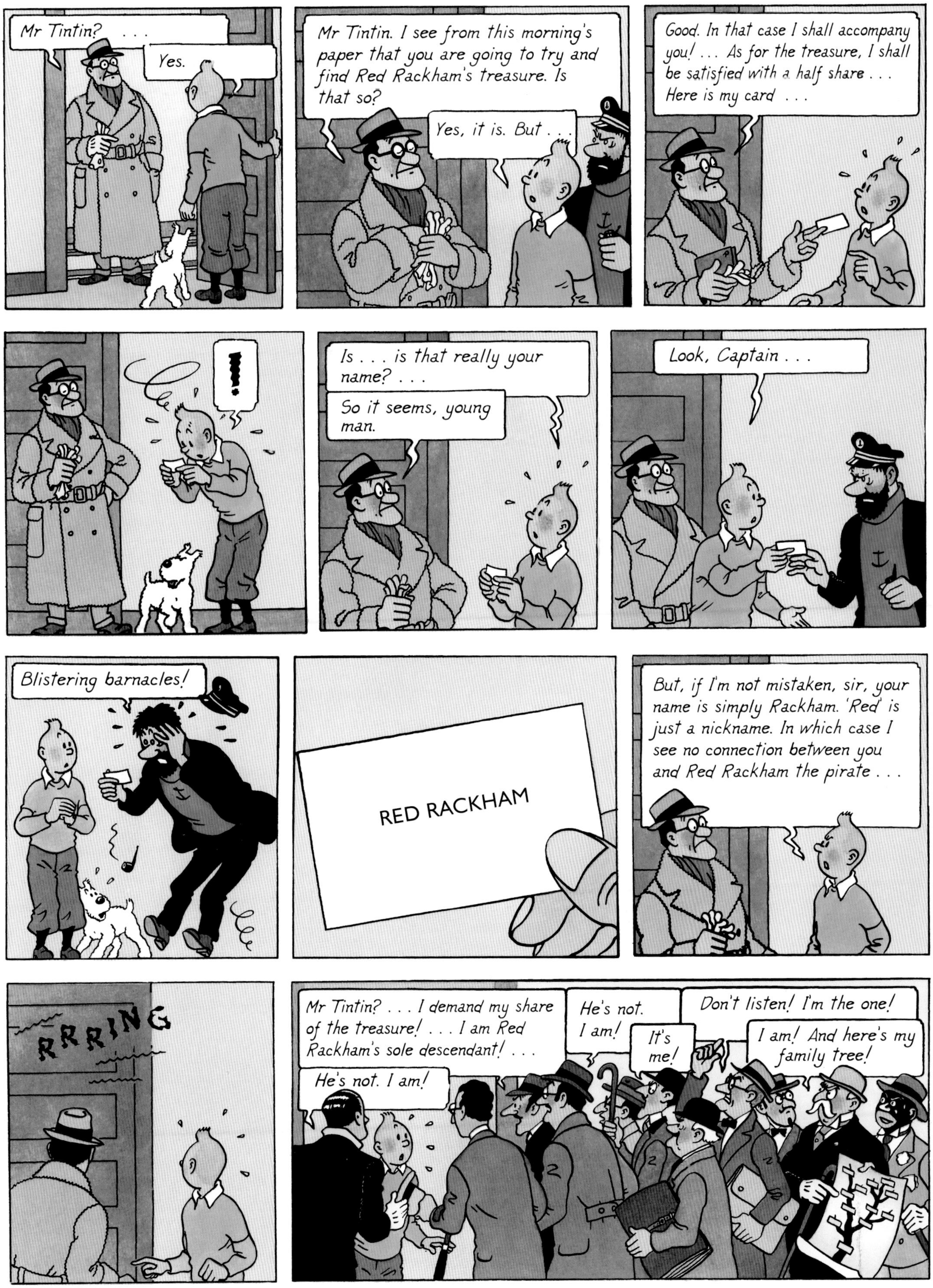
Mr Tintin? . . .
Yes.
Mr Tintin. I see from this morning's paper that you are going to try and find Red Rackham's treasure. Is that so?
Yes, it is. But . . .
Good. In that case I shall accompany you! . . . As for the treasure, I shall be satisfied with a half share . . . Here is my card . . .
!
Is . . . is that really your name? . . .
So it seems, young man.
Look, Captain . . .
Blistering barnacles!
RED RACKHAM
But, if I'm not mistaken, sir, your name is simply Rackham. 'Red' is just a nickname. In which case I see no connection between you and Red Rackham the pirate . . .
RRRING
Mr Tintin? . . . I demand my share of the treasure! . . . I am Red Rackham's sole descendant! . . .
He's not. I am!
He's not. I am!
It's me!
Don't listen! I'm the one!
I am! And here's my family tree!

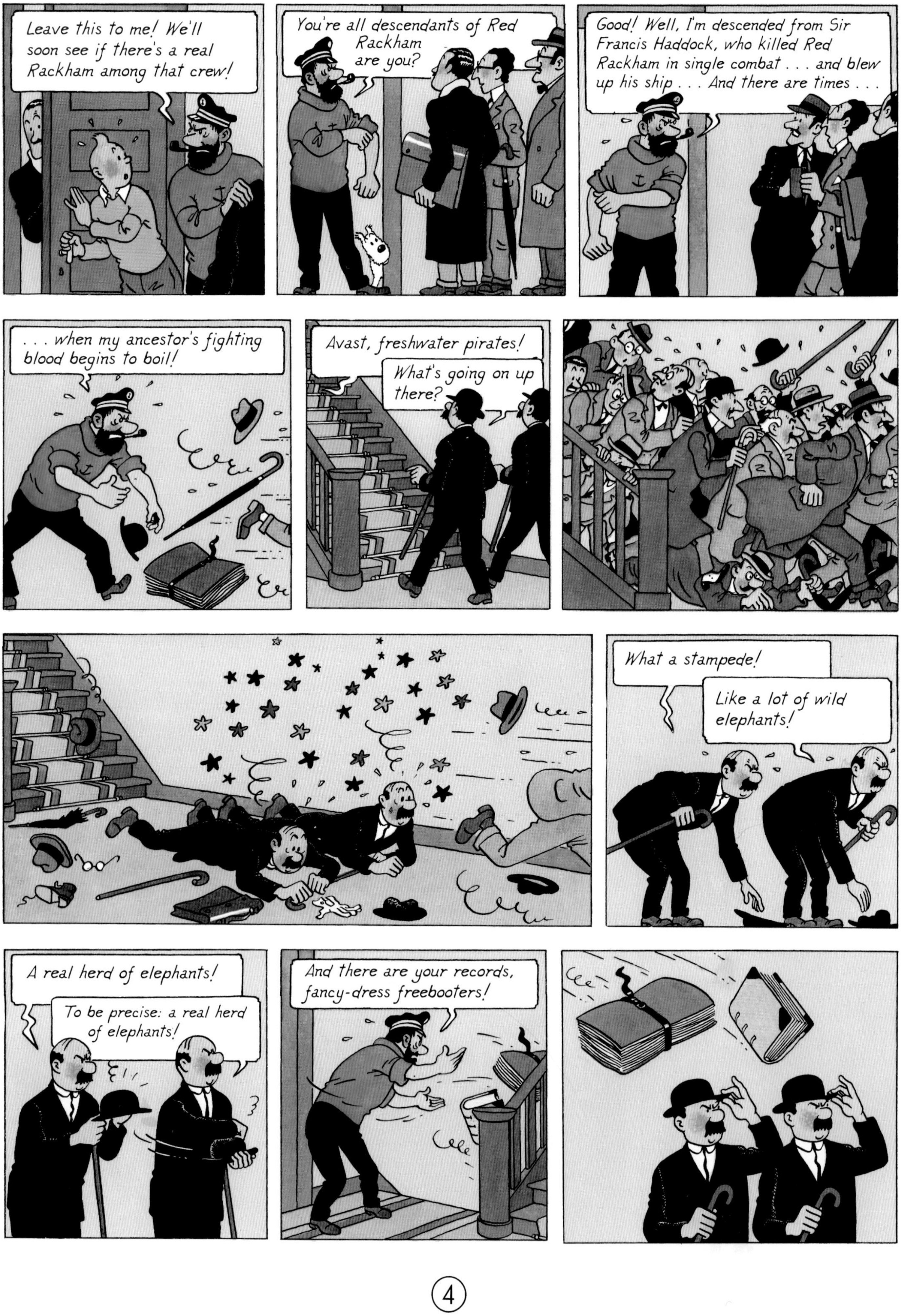
Leave this to me! We'll soon see if there's a real Rackham among that crew!
You're all descendants of Red Rackham are you?
Good! Well, I'm descended from Sir Francis Haddock, who killed Red Rackham in single combat . . . and blew up his ship . . . And there are times . . .
. . . when my ancestor's fighting blood begins to boil!
Avast, freshwater pirates!
What's going on up there?
What a stampede!
Like a lot of wild elephants!
A real herd of elephants!
To be precise: a real herd of elephants!
And there are your records, fancy-dress freebooters!

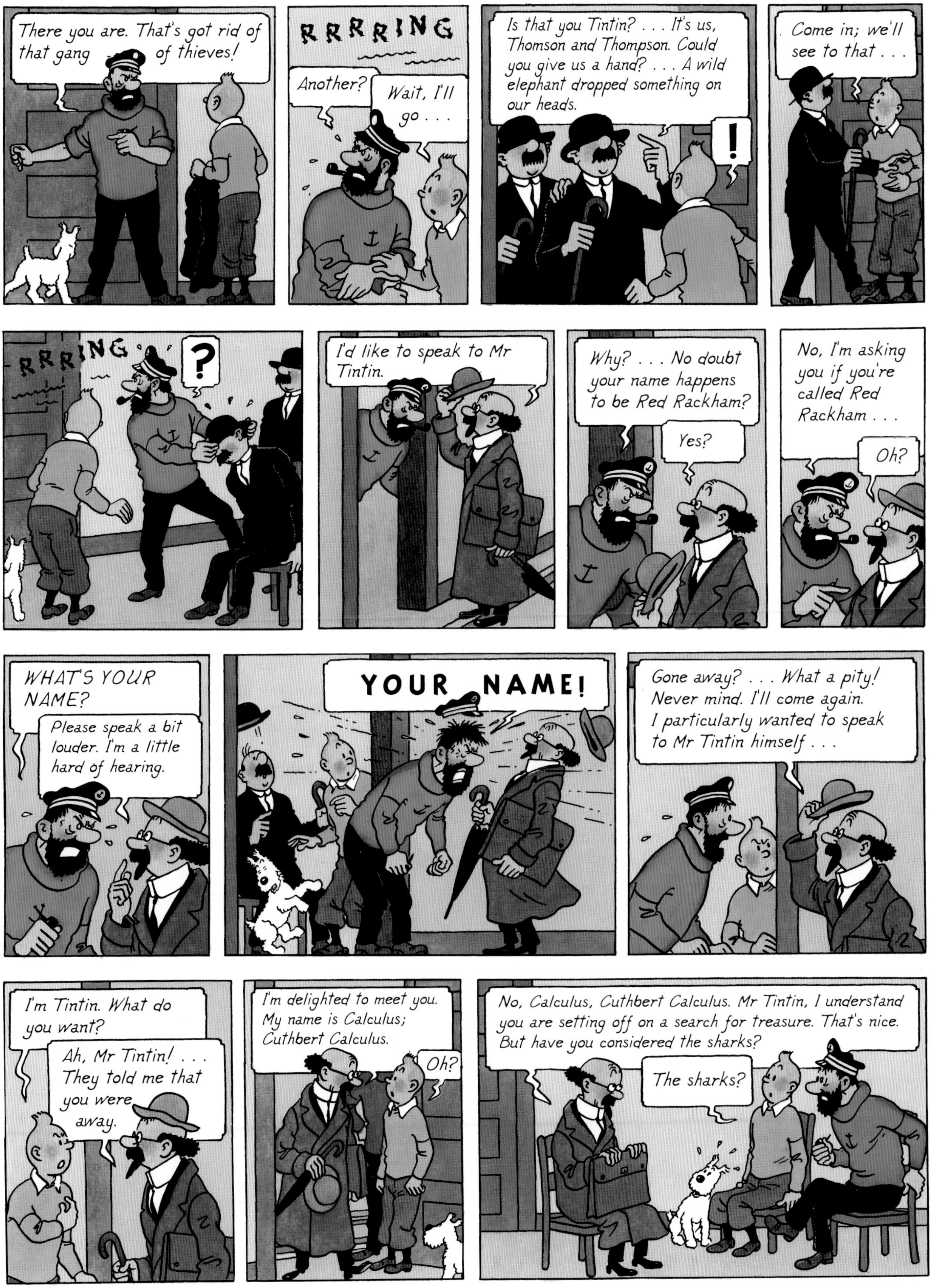
There you are. That's got rid of that gang of thieves!
RRRRING
Another?
Wait, I'll go . . .
Is that you Tintin? . . . It's us, Thomson and Thompson. Could you give us a hand? . . . A wild elephant dropped something on our heads.
!
Come in; we'll see to that . . .
RRRRING
?
I'd like to speak to Mr Tintin.
Why? . . . No doubt your name happens to be Red Rackham?
Yes?
No, I'm asking you if you're called Red Rackham . . .
Oh?
WHAT'S YOUR NAME?
Please speak a bit louder. I'm a little hard of hearing.
YOUR NAME!
Gone away? . . . What a pity! Never mind. I'll come again. I particularly wanted to speak to Mr Tintin himself . . .
I'm Tintin. What do you want?
Ah, Mr Tintin! . . . They told me that you were away.
I'm delighted to meet you. My name is Calculus; Cuthbert Calculus.
Oh?
No, Calculus, Cuthbert Calculus. Mr Tintin, I understand you are setting off on a search for treasure. That's nice. But have you considered the sharks?
The sharks?

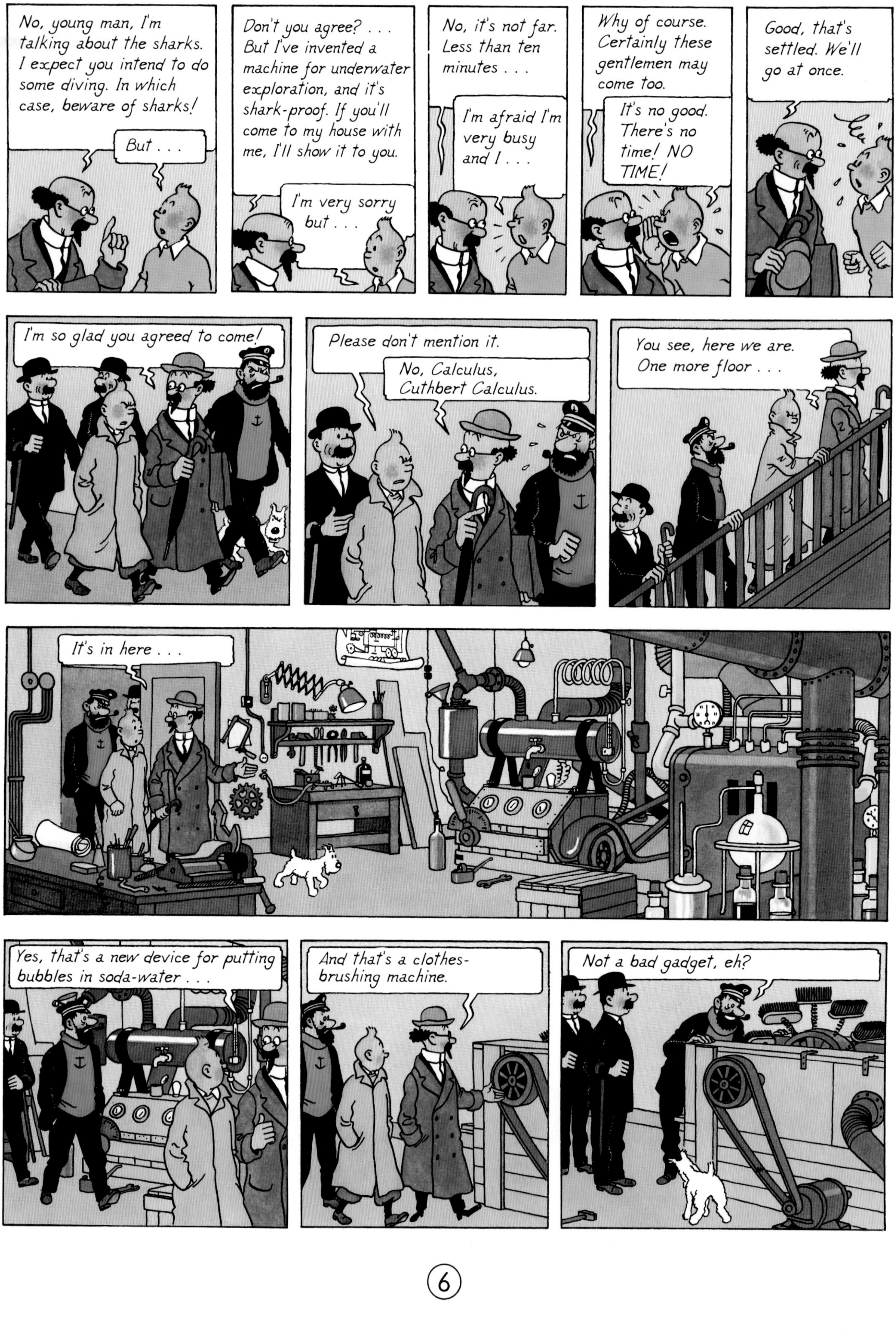
No, young man, I'm talking about the sharks. I expect you intend to do some diving. In which case, beware of sharks!
But . . .
Don't you agree? . . . But I've invented a machine for underwater exploration, and it's shark-proof. If you'll come to my house with me, I'll show it to you.
I'm very sorry but . . .
No, it's not far. Less than ten minutes . . .
I'm afraid I'm very busy and I . . .
Why of course. Certainly these gentlemen may come too.
It's no good. There's no time! NO TIME!
Good, that's settled. We'll go at once.
I'm so glad you agreed to come!
Please don't mention it.
No, Calculus, Cuthbert Calculus.
You see, here we are. One more floor . . .
It's in here . . .
Yes, that's a new device for putting bubbles in soda-water . . .
And that's a clothes-brushing machine.
Not a bad gadget, eh?

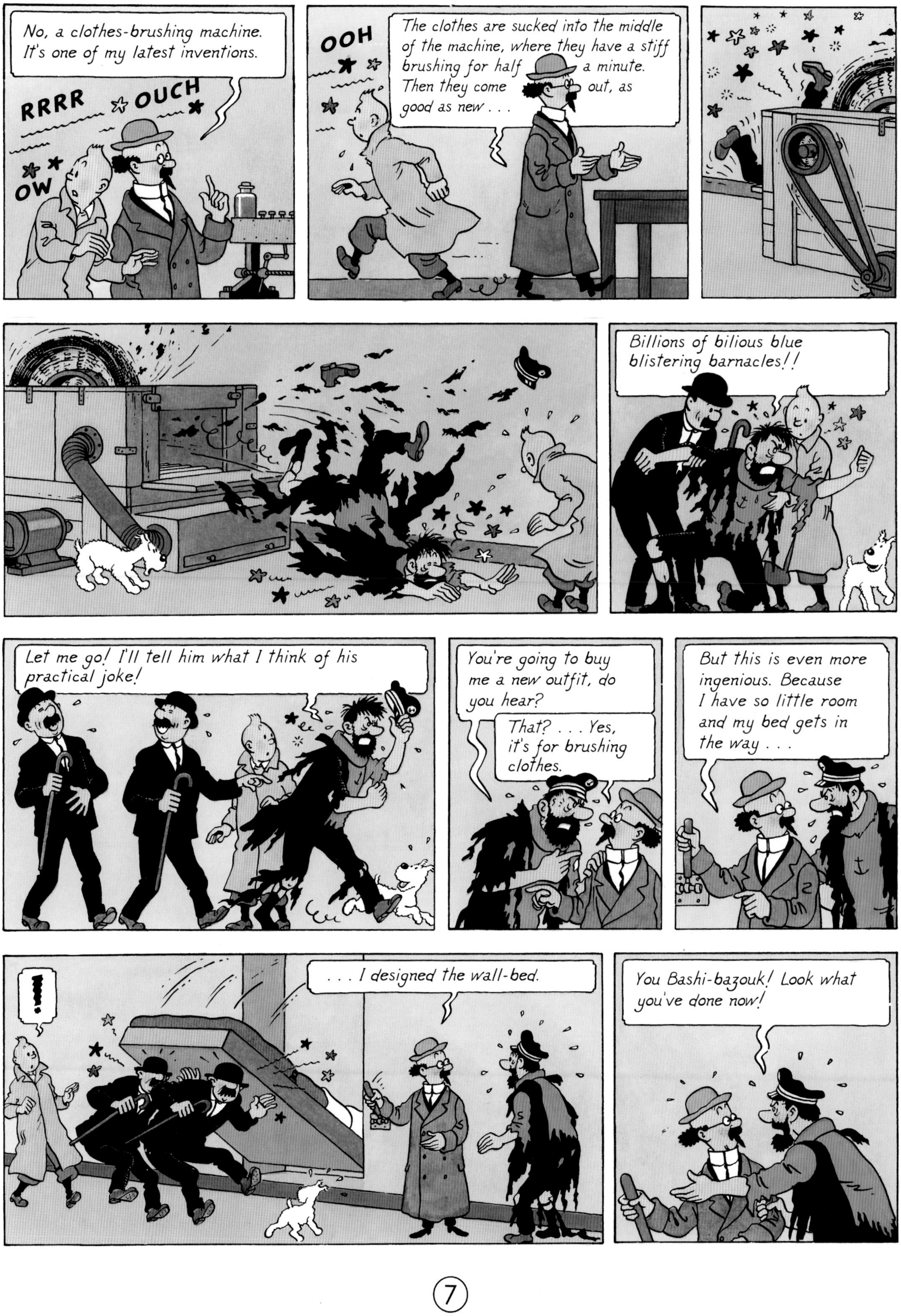
No, a clothes-brushing machine. It's one of my latest inventions.
RRRR
OUCH
OW
OOH
The clothes are sucked into the middle of the machine, where they have a stiff brushing for half a minute. Then they come out, as good as new . . .
Billions of bilious blue blistering barnacles!!
Let me go! I'll tell him what I think of his practical joke!
You're going to buy me a new outfit, do you hear?
That? . . . Yes, it's for brushing clothes.
But this is even more ingenious. Because I have so little room and my bed gets in the way . . .
!
. . . I designed the wall-bed.
You Bashi-bazouk! Look what you've done now!

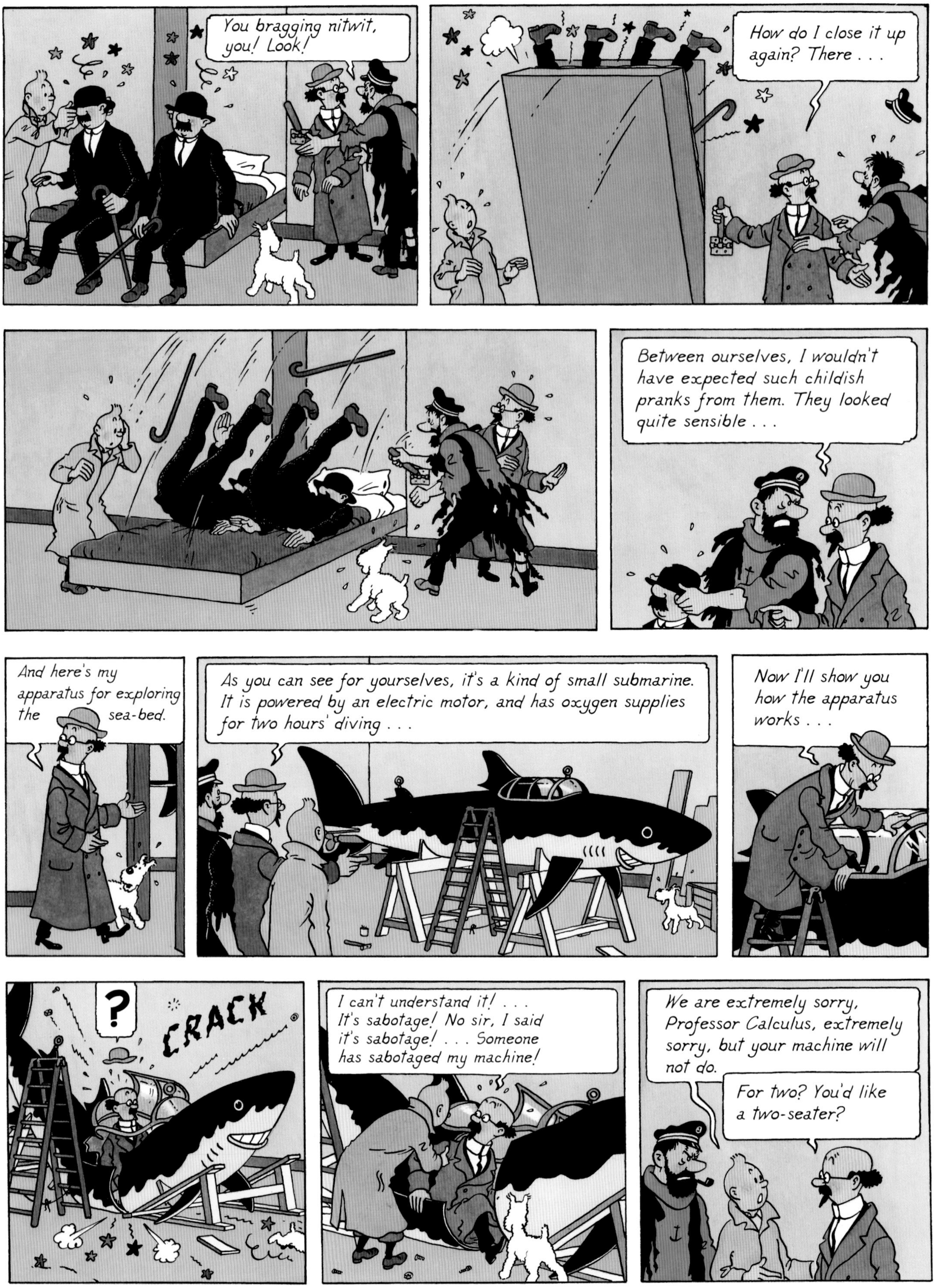
You bragging nitwit, you! Look!
How do I close it up again? There . . .
Between ourselves, I wouldn't have expected such childish pranks from them. They looked quite sensible . . .
And here's my apparatus for exploring the sea-bed.
As you can see for yourselves, it's a kind of small submarine. It is powered by an electric motor, and has oxygen supplies for two hours' diving . . .
Now I'll show you how the apparatus works . . .
?
CRACK
I can't understand it! . . . It's sabotage! No sir, I said it's sabotage! . . . Someone has sabotaged my machine!
We are extremely sorry, Professor Calculus, extremely sorry, but your machine will not do.
For two? You'd like a two-seater?

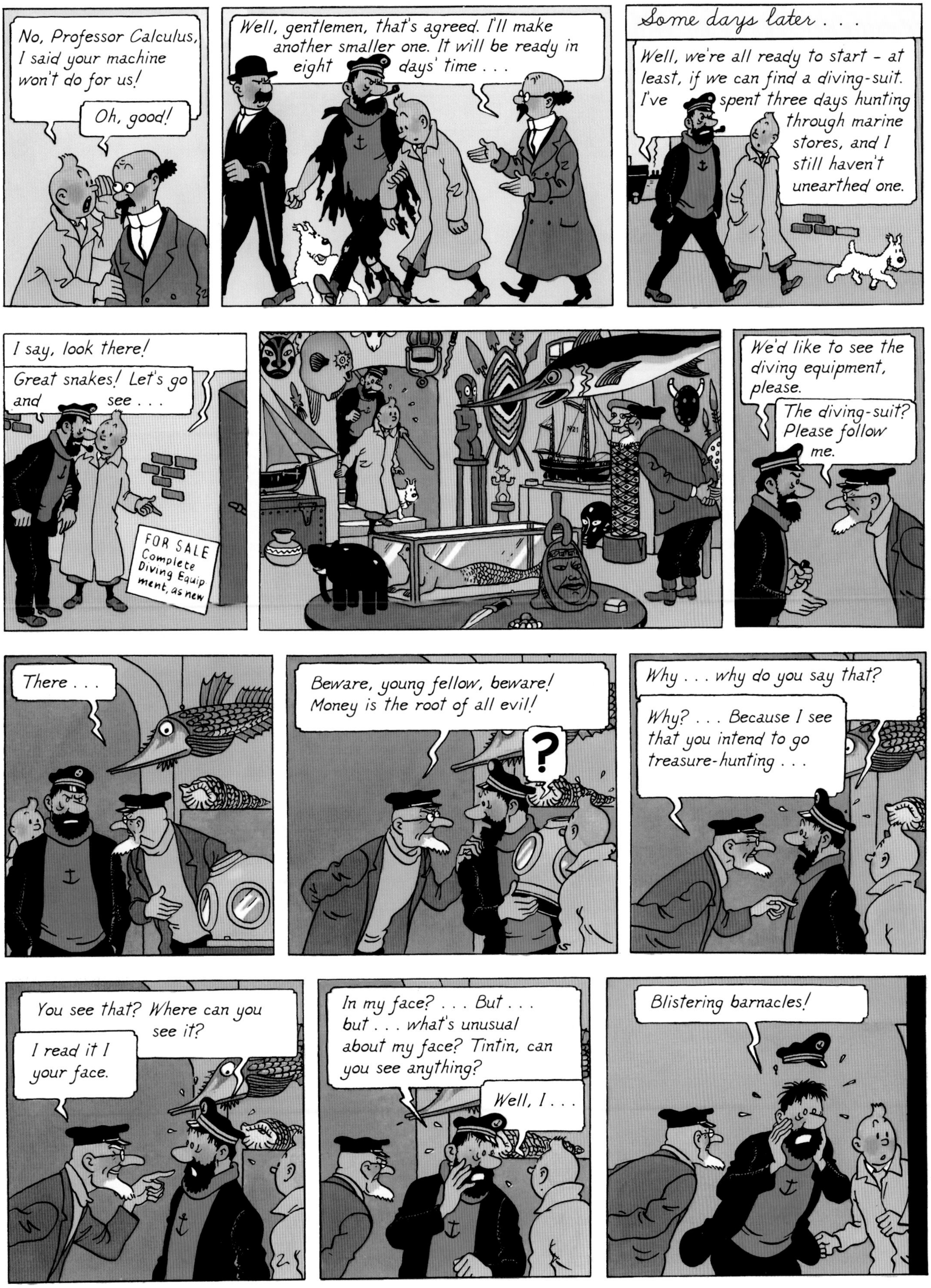
No, Professor Calculus, I said your machine won't do for us!
Oh, good!
Well, gentlemen, that's agreed. I'll make another smaller one. It will be ready in eight days' time . . .
Some days later . . .
Well, we're all ready to start - at least, if we can find a diving-suit. I've spent three days hunting through marine stores, and I still haven't unearthed one.
I say, look there!
Great snakes! Let's go and see . . .
FOR SALE Complete Diving Equipment, as new
We'd like to see the diving equipment, please.
The diving-suit? Please follow me.
There . . .
Beware, young fellow, beware! Money is the root of all evil!
?
Why . . . why do you say that?
Why? . . . Because I see that you intend to go treasure-hunting . . .
You see that? Where can you see it?
I read it I your face.
In my face? . . . But . . . but . . . what's unusual about my face? Tintin, can you see anything?
Well, I . . .
Blistering barnacles!

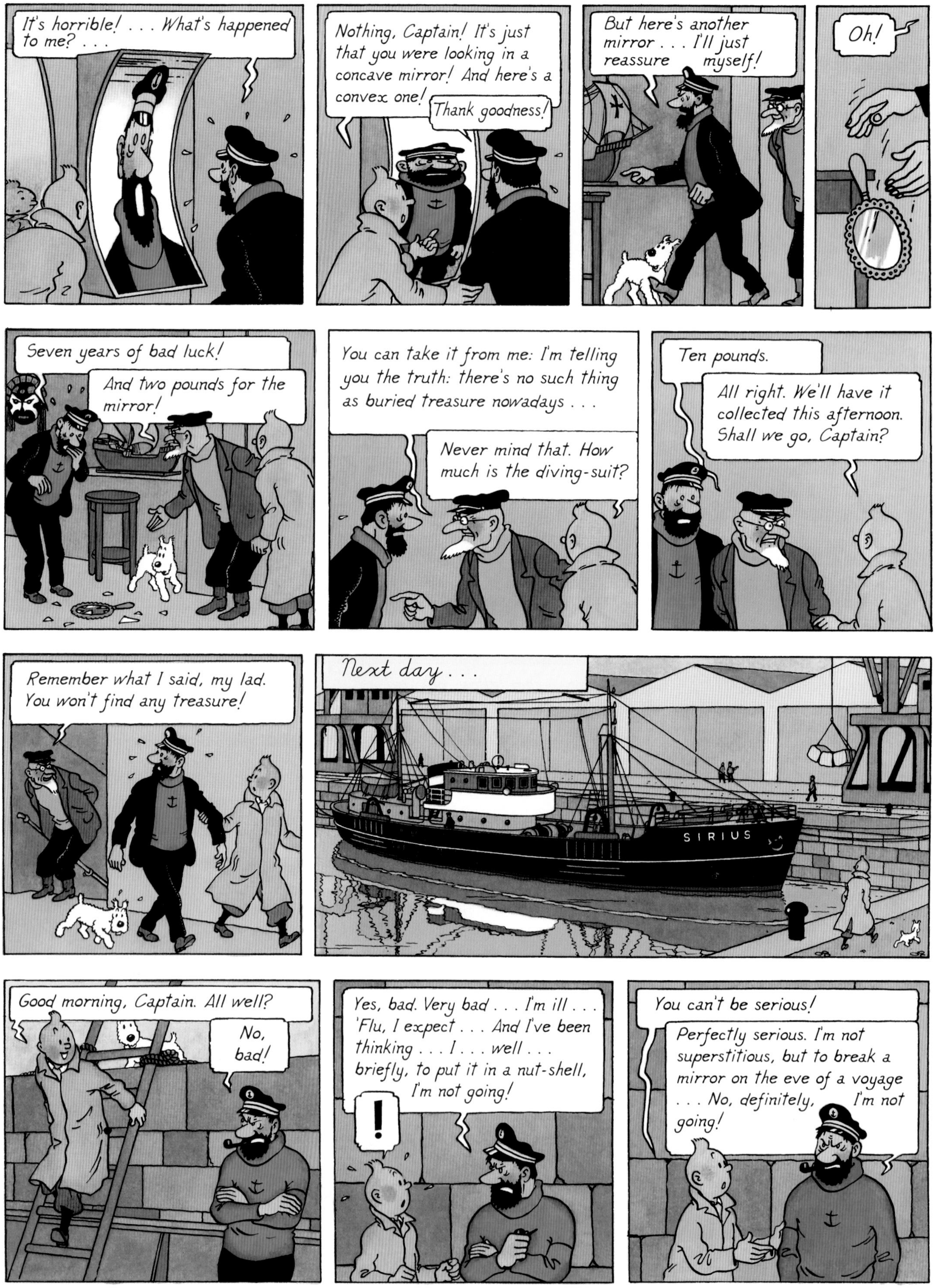

It's horrible! . . . What's happened to me? . . .
Nothing, Captain! It's just that you were looking in a concave mirror! And here's a convex one!
Thank goodness!
But here's another mirror . . . I'll just reassure myself!
Oh!
Seven years of bad luck!
And two pounds for the mirror!
You can take it from me: I'm telling you the truth: there's no such thing as buried treasure nowadays . . .
Never mind that. How much is the diving-suit?
Ten pounds.
All right. We'll have it collected this afternoon. Shall we go, Captain?
Remember what I said, my lad. You won't find any treasure!
Next day . . .
SIRIUS
Good morning, Captain. All well?
No, bad!
Yes, bad. Very bad . . . I'm ill . . . 'Flu, I expect . . . And I've been thinking . . . I . . . well . . . briefly, to put it in a nut-shell, I'm not going!
!
You can't be serious!
Perfectly serious. I'm not superstitious, but to break a mirror on the eve of a voyage . . . No, definitely, I'm not going!

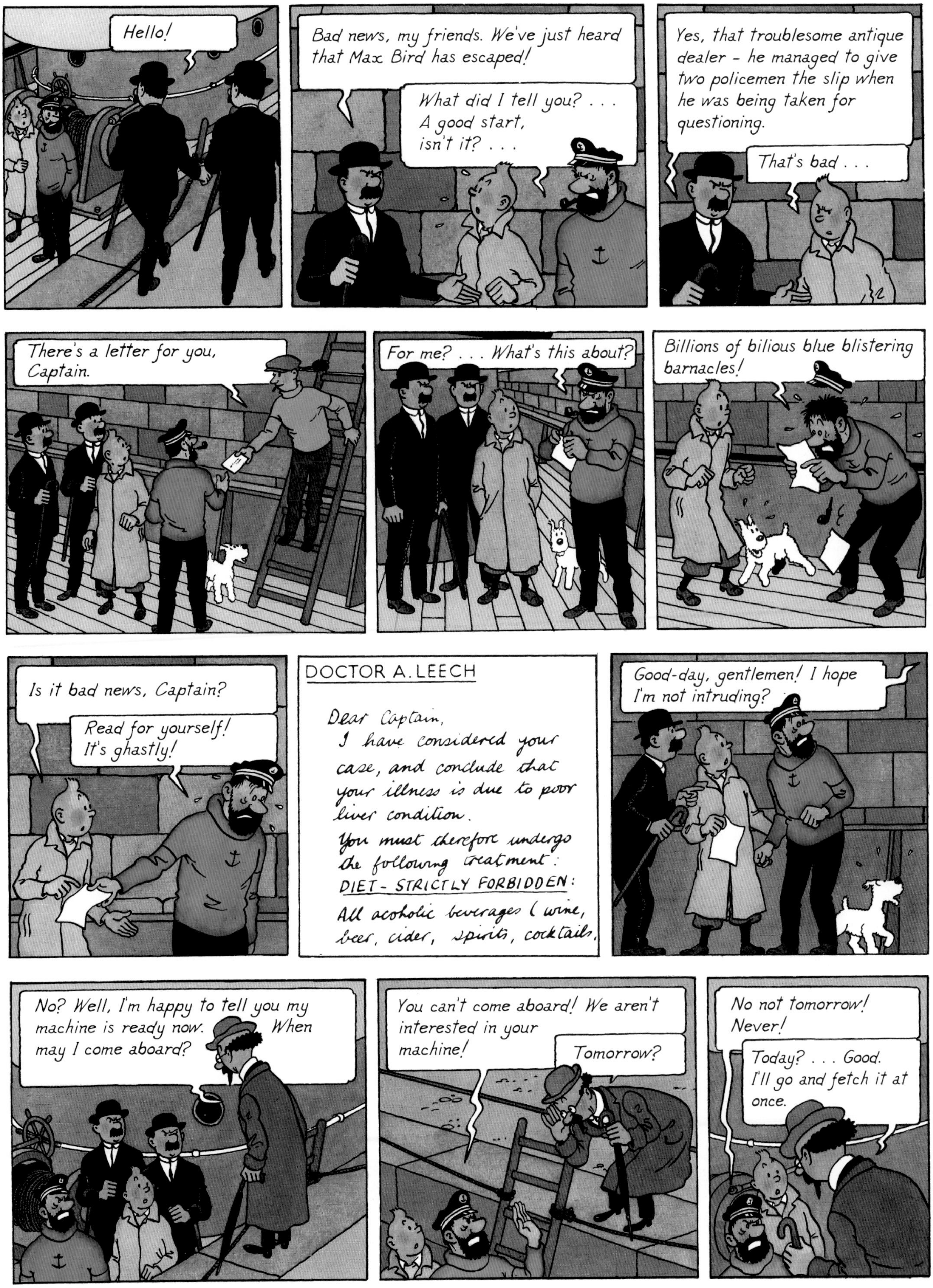

Hello!
Bad news, my friends. We've just heard that Max Bird has escaped!
What did I tell you? . . . A good start, isn't it? . . .
Yes, that troublesome antique dealer - he managed to give two policemen the slip when he was being taken for questioning.
That's bad . . .
There's a letter for you, Captain.
For me? . . . What's this about?
Billions of bilious blue blistering barnacles!
Is it bad news, Captain?
Read for yourself! It's ghastly!
DOCTOR A. LEECH
Dear Captain,
I have considered your case, and conclude that your illness is due to poor liver condition.
You must therefore undergo the following treatment:
DIET - STRICTLY FORBIDDEN:
All acoholic beverages (wine, beer, cider, spirits, cocktails,
Good-day, gentlemen! I hope I'm not intruding?
No? Well, I'm happy to tell you my machine is ready now. When may I come aboard?
You can't come aboard! We aren't interested in your machine!
Tomorrow?
No not tomorrow! Never!
Today? . . . Good. I'll go and fetch it at once.

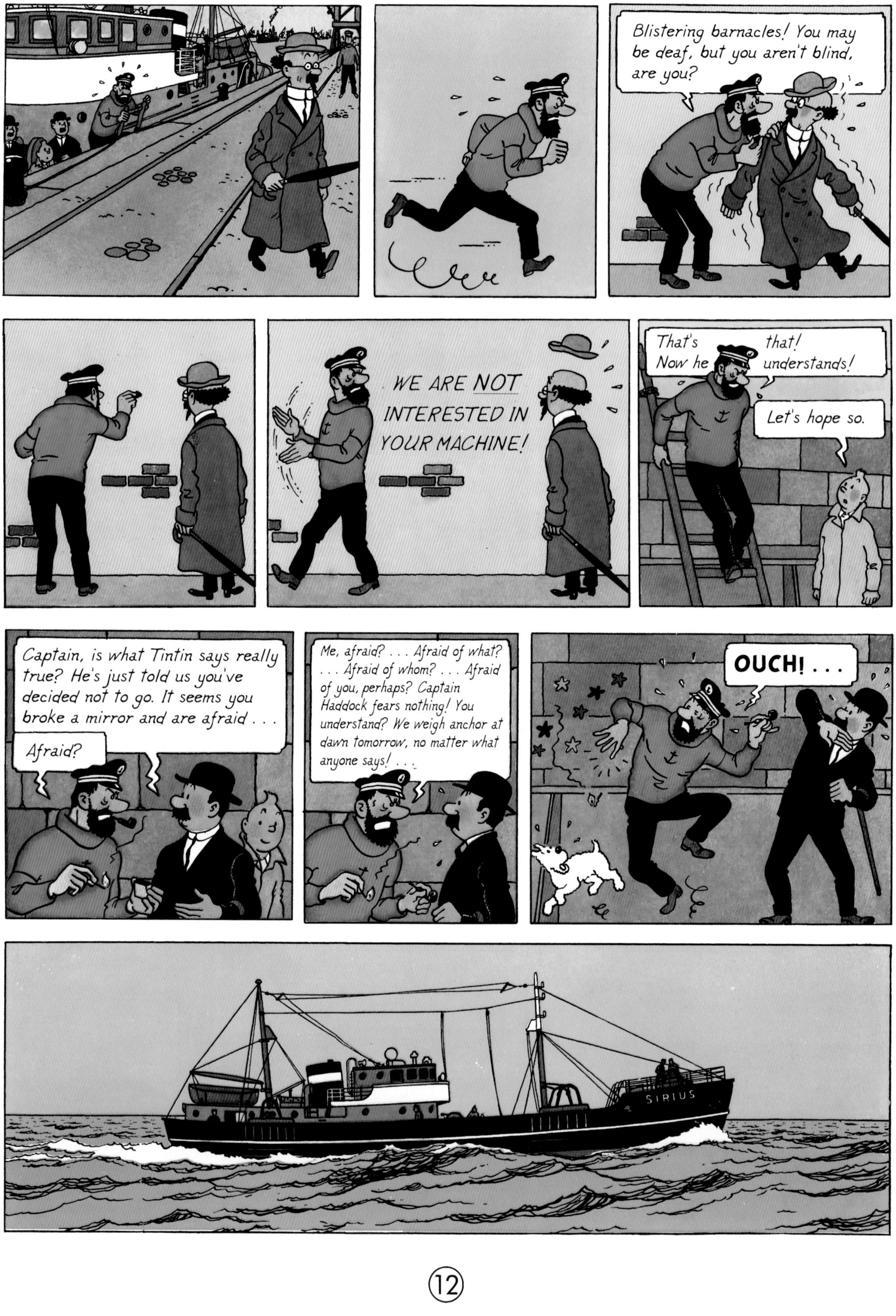

Blistering barnacles! You may be deaf, but you aren't blind, are you?
WE ARE NOT INTERESTED IN YOUR MACHINE!
That's that! Now he understands!
Let's hope so.
Captain, is what Tintin says really true? He's just told us you've decided not to go. It seems you broke a mirror and are afraid . . .
Afraid?
Me, afraid? . . . Afraid of what? . . . Afraid of whom? . . . Afraid of you, perhaps? Captain Haddock fears nothing! You understand? We weigh anchor at dawn tomorrow, no matter what anyone says! . . .
OUCH! . . .
SIRIUS

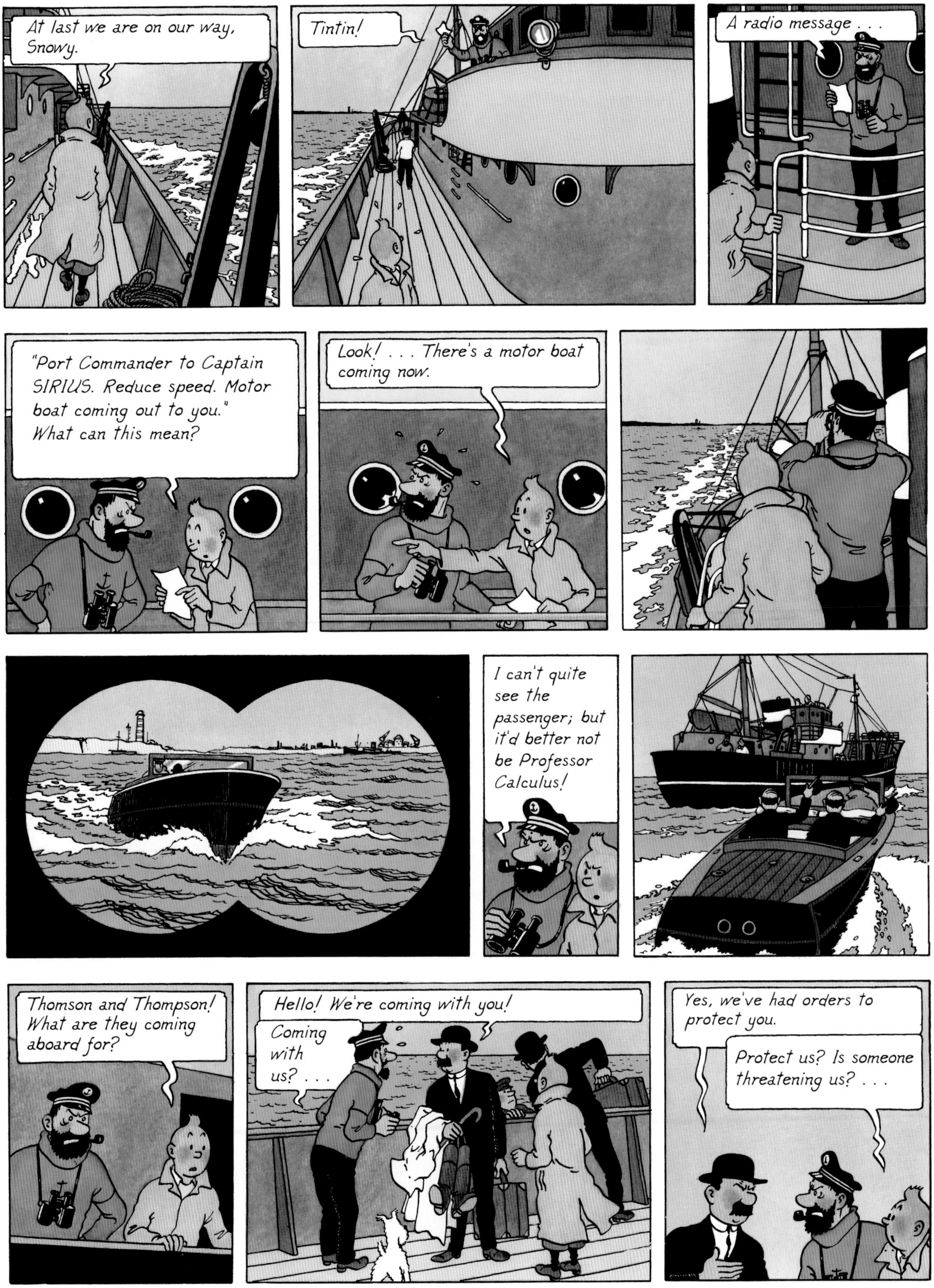

At last we are on our way, Snowy.
Tintin!
A radio message . . .
"Port Commander to Captain SIRIUS. Reduce speed. Motor boat coming out to you." What can this mean?
Look! . . . There's a motor boat coming now.
I can't quite see the passenger; but it'd better not be Professor Calculus!
Thomson and Thompson! What are they coming aboard for?
Hello! We're coming with you!
Coming with us? . . .
Yes, we've had orders to protect you.
Protect us? Is someone threatening us? . . .

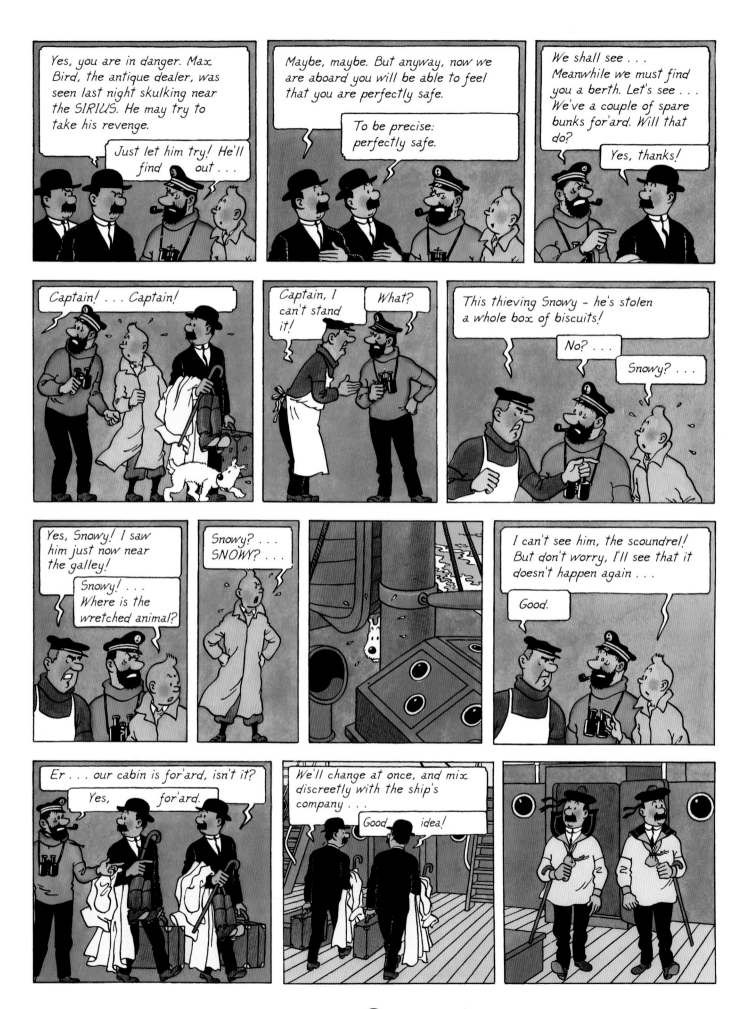

Yes, you are in danger. Max Bird, the antique dealer, was seen last night skulking near the SIRIUS. He may try to take his revenge.

Just let him try! He'll find out . . .

Maybe, maybe. But anyway, now we are aboard you will be able to feel that you are perfectly safe.

To be precise: perfectly safe.

We shall see . . . Meanwhile we must find you a berth. Let's see . . . We've a couple of spare bunks for'ard. Will that do?

Yes, thanks!

Captain! . . . Captain!

Captain, I can't stand it!

What?

This thieving Snowy - he's stolen a whole box of biscuits!

No? . . .

Snowy? . . .

Yes, Snowy! I saw him just now near the galley!

Snowy! . . . Where is the wretched animal?

Snowy? . . . SNOWY? . . .

I can't see him, the scoundrel! But don't worry, I'll see that it doesn't happen again . . .

Good.

Er . . . our cabin is for'ard, isn't it?

Yes, for'ard.

We'll change at once, and mix discreetly with the ship's company . . .

Good idea!

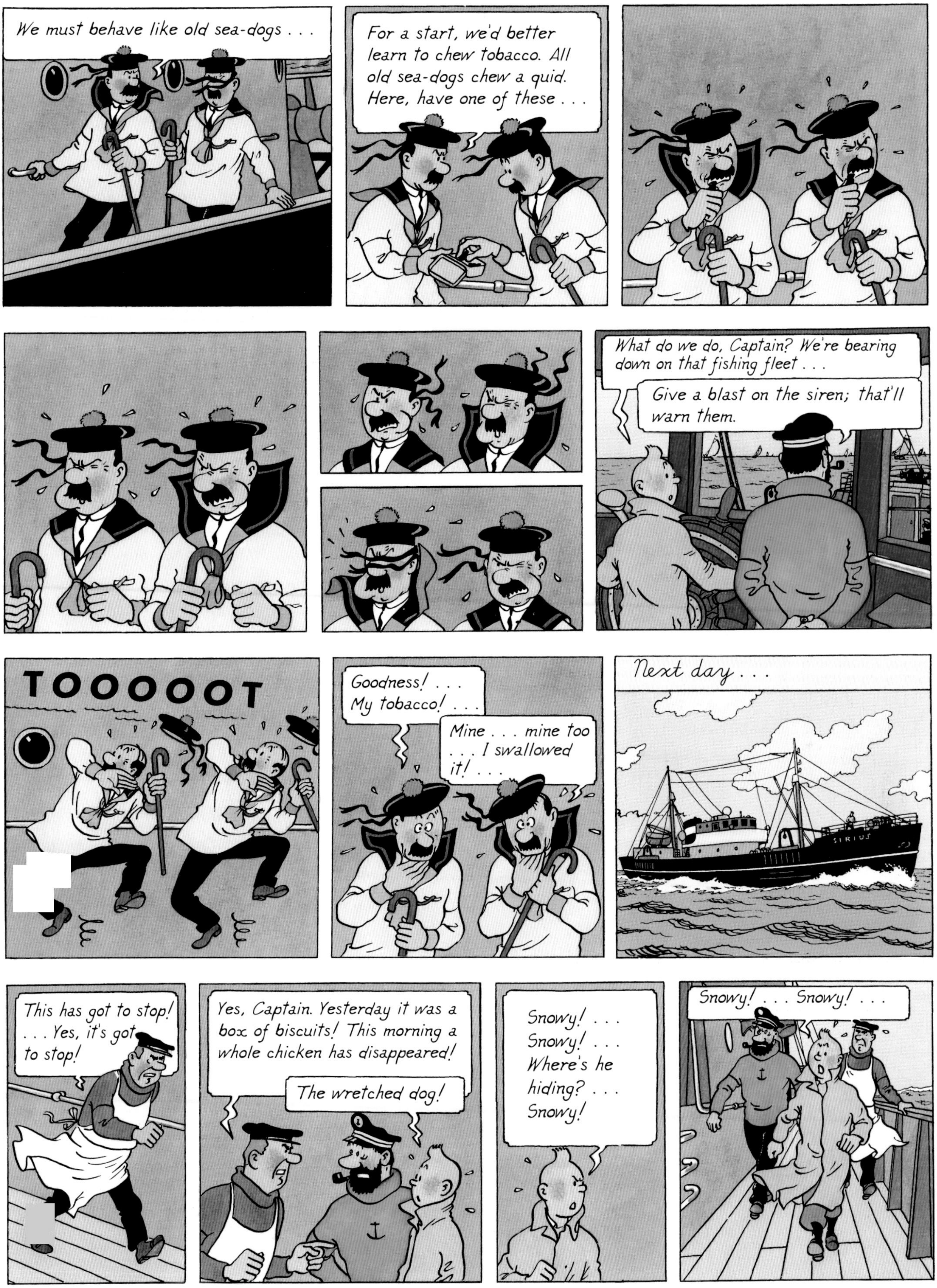
We must behave like old sea-dogs . . .
For a start, we'd better learn to chew tobacco. All old sea-dogs chew a quid. Here, have one of these . . .
What do we do, Captain? We're bearing down on that fishing fleet . . .
Give a blast on the siren; that'll warn them.
TOOOOOT
Goodness! . . . My tobacco! . . .
Mine . . . mine too . . . I swallowed it! . . .
Next day . . .
SIRIUS
This has got to stop! . . . Yes, it's got to stop!
Yes, Captain. Yesterday it was a box of biscuits! This morning a whole chicken has disappeared!
The wretched dog!
Snowy! . . . Snowy! . . . Where's he hiding? . . . Snowy!
Snowy! . . . Snowy! . . .

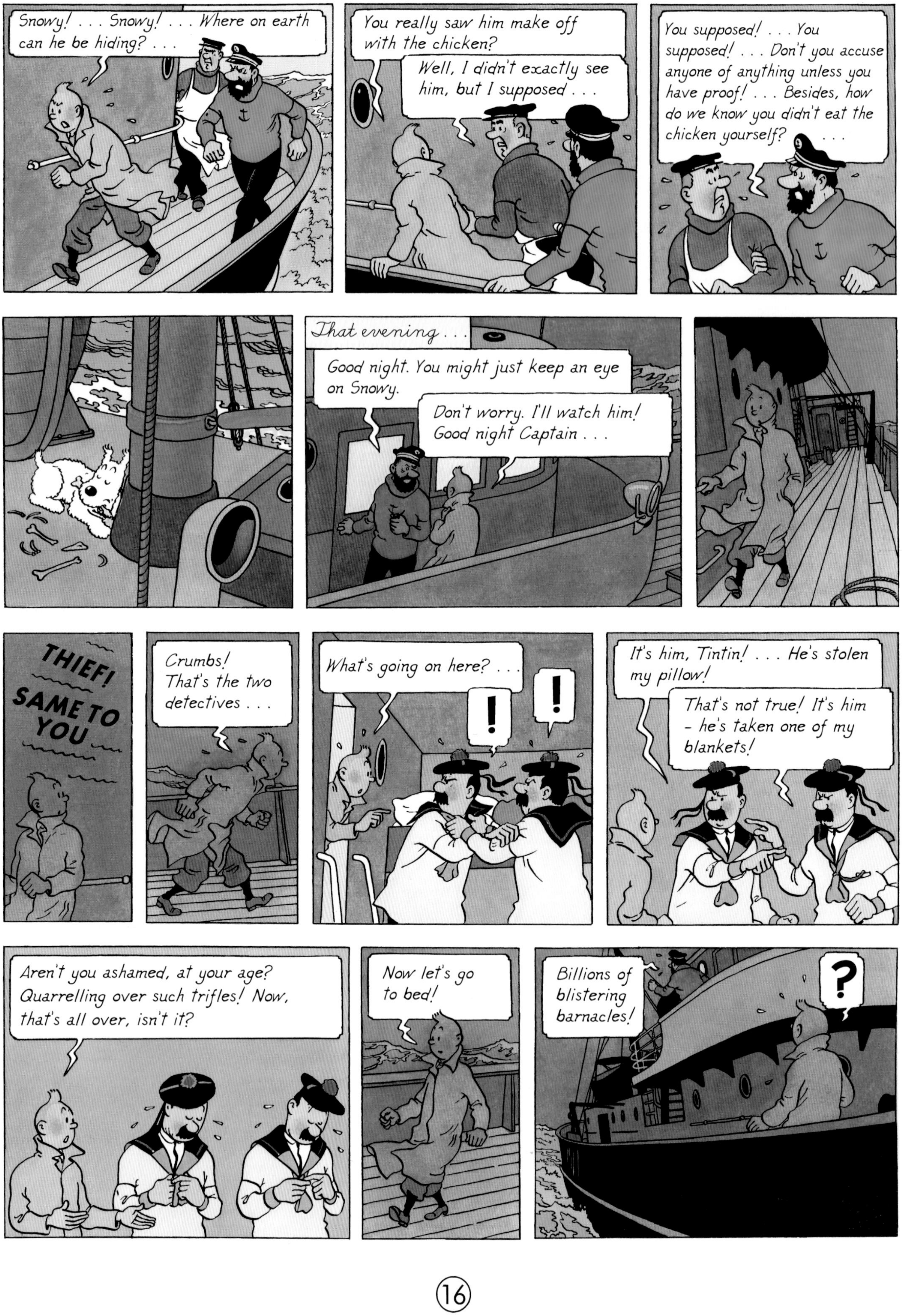
Snowy! . . . Snowy! . . . Where on earth can he be hiding? . . .
You really saw him make off with the chicken?
Well, I didn't exactly see him, but I supposed . . .
You supposed! . . . You supposed! . . . Don't you accuse anyone of anything unless you have proof! . . . Besides, how do we know you didn't eat the chicken yourself? . . .
That evening . . .
Good night. You might just keep an eye on Snowy.
Don't worry. I'll watch him! Good night Captain . . .
THIEF!
SAME TO YOU
Crumbs! That's the two detectives . . .
What's going on here? . . .
!
!
It's him, Tintin! . . . He's stolen my pillow!
That's not true! It's him – he's taken one of my blankets!
Aren't you ashamed, at your age? Quarrelling over such trifles! Now, that's all over, isn't it?
Now let's go to bed!
Billions of blistering barnacles!
?

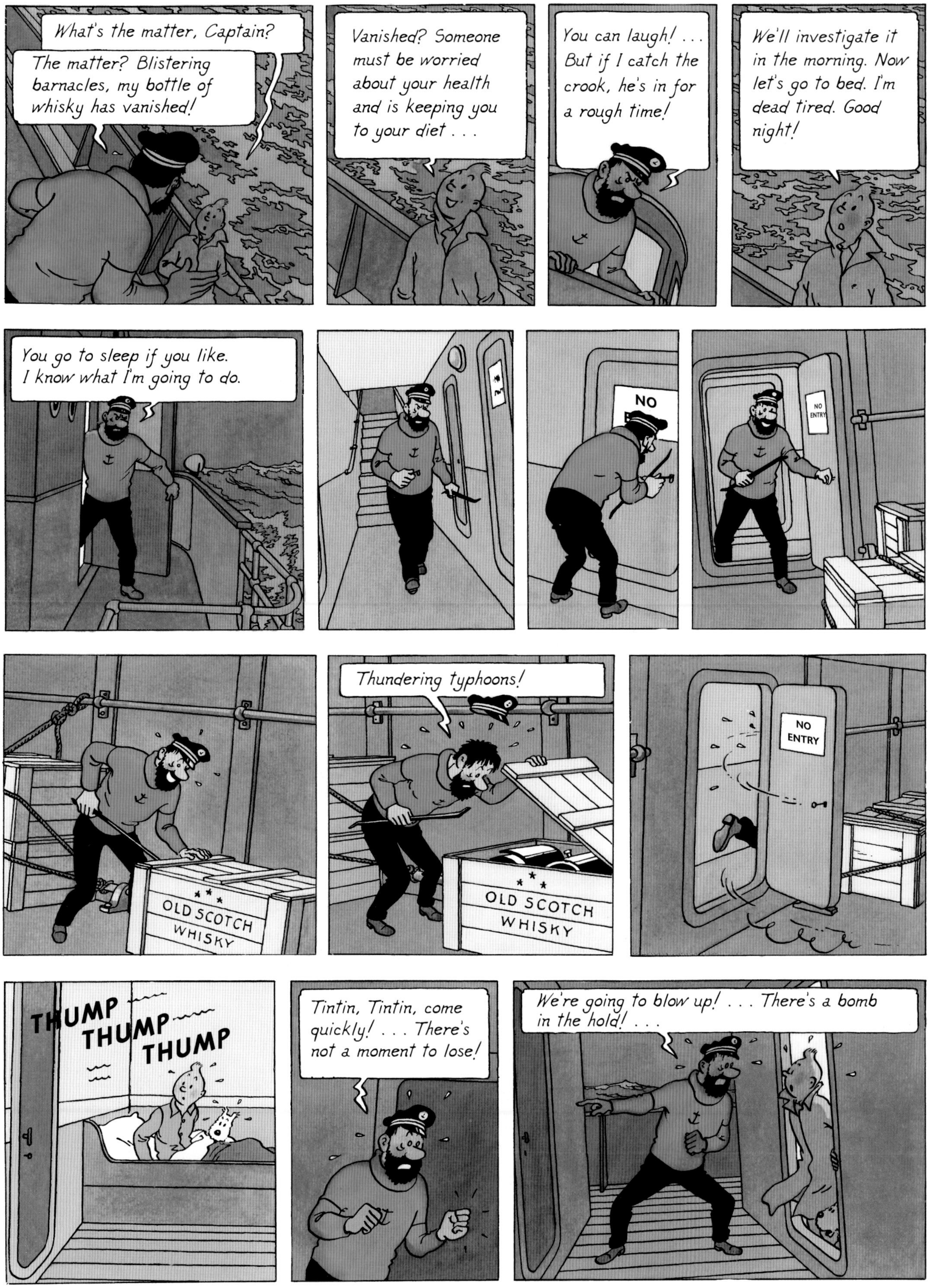
What's the matter, Captain?
The matter? Blistering barnacles, my bottle of whisky has vanished!
Vanished? Someone must be worried about your health and is keeping you to your diet . . .
You can laugh! . . . But if I catch the crook, he's in for a rough time!
We'll investigate it in the morning. Now let's go to bed. I'm dead tired. Good night!
You go to sleep if you like. I know what I'm going to do.
NO
NO ENTRY
OLD SCOTCH WHISKY
Thundering typhoons!
OLD SCOTCH WHISKY
NO ENTRY
THUMP THUMP THUMP
Tintin, Tintin, come quickly! . . . There's not a moment to lose!
We're going to blow up! . . . There's a bomb in the hold! . . .

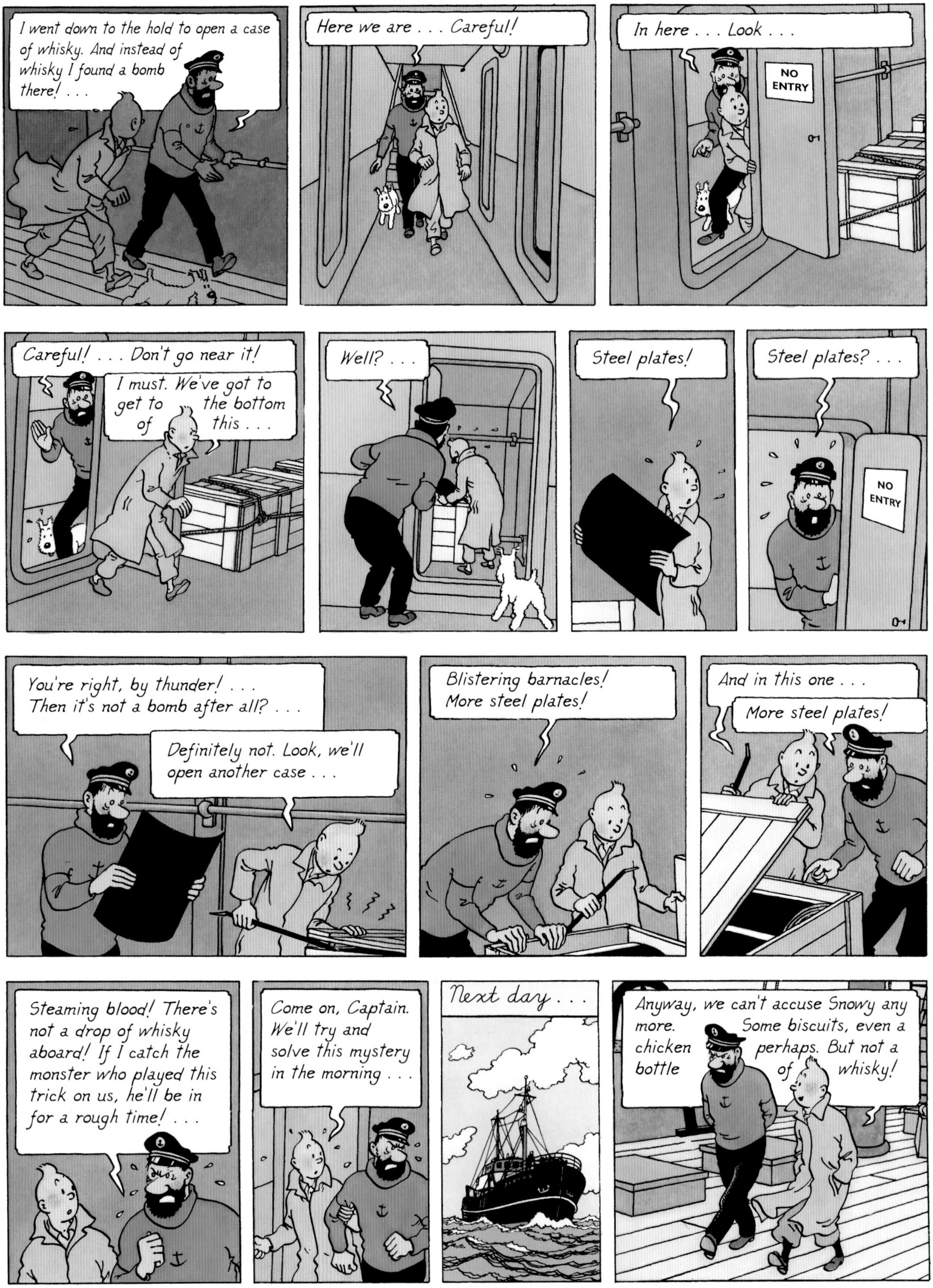
I went down to the hold to open a case of whisky. And instead of whisky I found a bomb there! . . .
Here we are . . . Careful!
In here . . . Look . . .
NO ENTRY
Careful! . . . Don't go near it!
I must. We've got to get to the bottom of this . . .
Well? . . .
Steel plates!
Steel plates? . . .
NO ENTRY
You're right, by thunder! . . . Then it's not a bomb after all? . . .
Definitely not. Look, we'll open another case . . .
Blistering barnacles! More steel plates!
And in this one . . .
More steel plates!
Steaming blood! There's not a drop of whisky aboard! If I catch the monster who played this trick on us, he'll be in for a rough time! . . .
Come on, Captain. We'll try and solve this mystery in the morning . . .
Next day . . .
Anyway, we can't accuse Snowy any more. Some biscuits, even a chicken perhaps. But not a bottle of whisky!

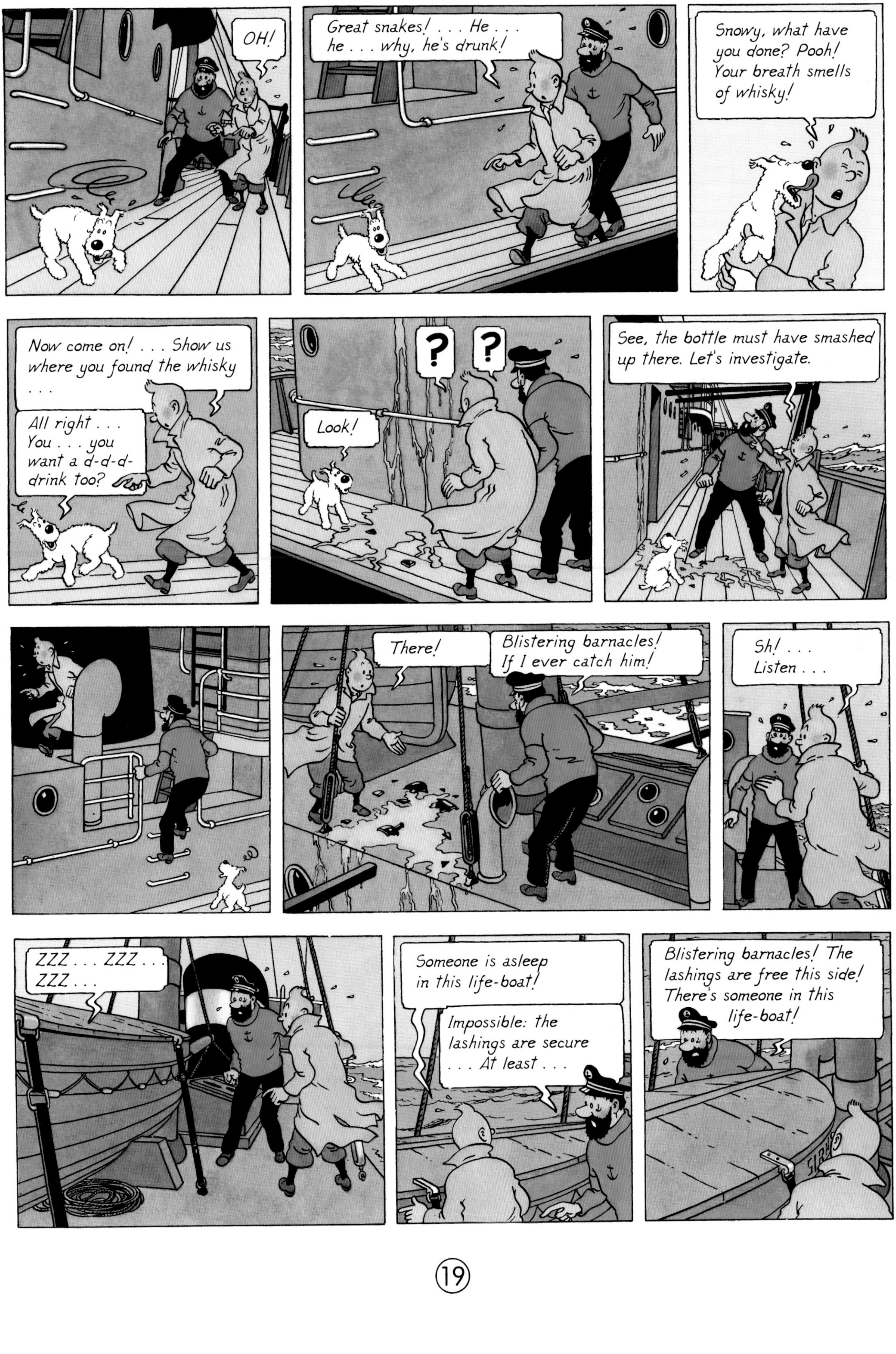
OH!
Great snakes! . . . He . . . he . . . why, he's drunk!
Snowy, what have you done? Pooh! Your breath smells of whisky!
Now come on! . . . Show us where you found the whisky . . .
All right . . . You . . . you want a d-d-d-drink too?
? ?
Look!
See, the bottle must have smashed up there. Let's investigate.
There!
Blistering barnacles! If I ever catch him!
Sh! . . . Listen . . .
ZZZ . . . ZZZ . . . ZZZ . . .
Someone is asleep in this life-boat!
Impossible: the lashings are secure . . . At least . . .
Blistering barnacles! The lashings are free this side! There's someone in this life-boat!

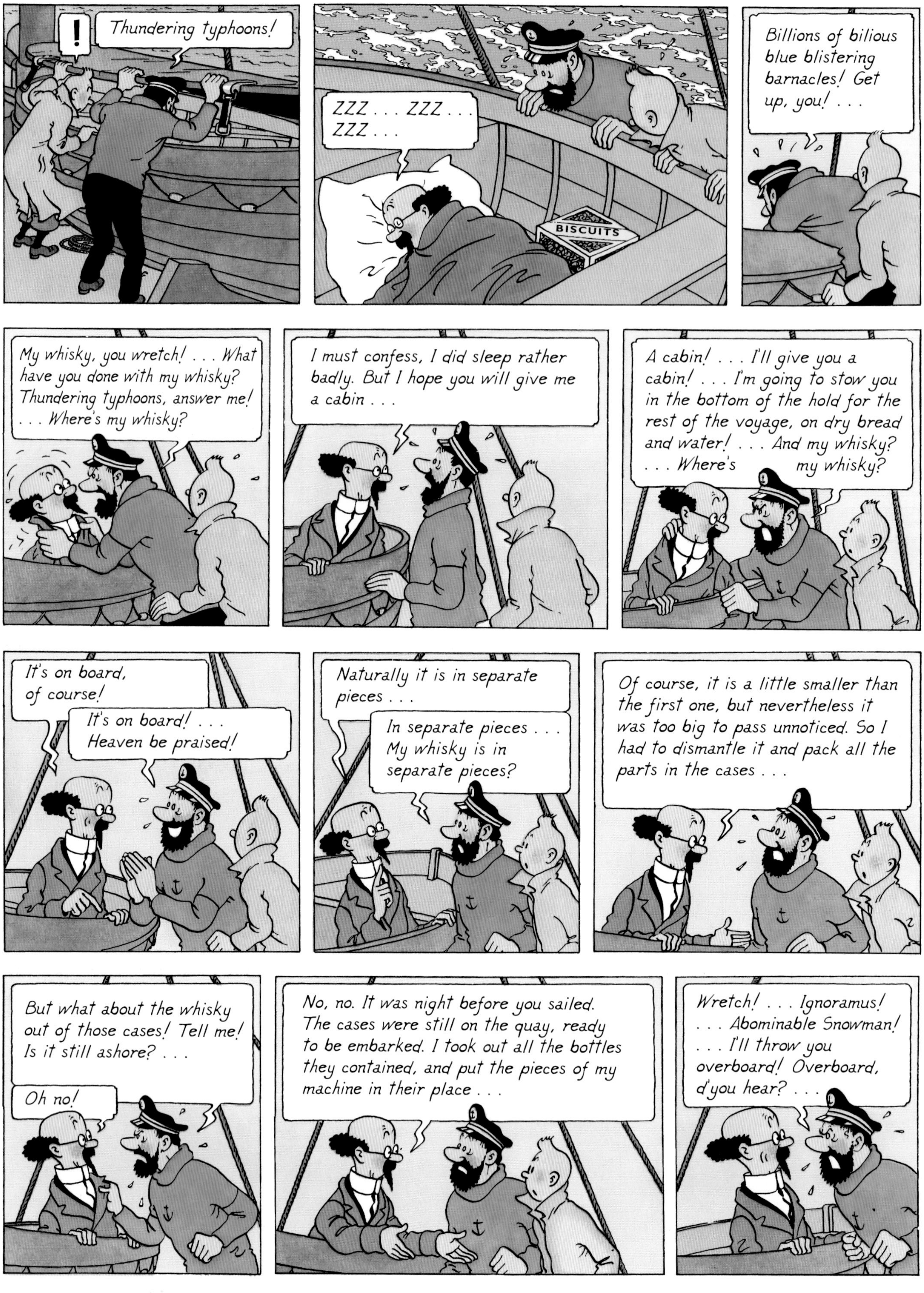
!
Thundering typhoons!
ZZZ . . . ZZZ . . . ZZZ . . .
BISCUITS
Billions of bilious blue blistering barnacles! Get up, you! . . .
My whisky, you wretch! . . . What have you done with my whisky? Thundering typhoons, answer me! . . . Where's my whisky?
I must confess, I did sleep rather badly. But I hope you will give me a cabin . . .
A cabin! . . . I'll give you a cabin! . . . I'm going to stow you in the bottom of the hold for the rest of the voyage, on dry bread and water! . . . And my whisky? . . . Where's my whisky?
It's on board, of course!
It's on board! . . . Heaven be praised!
Naturally it is in separate pieces . . .
In separate pieces . . . My whisky is in separate pieces?
Of course, it is a little smaller than the first one, but nevertheless it was too big to pass unnoticed. So I had to dismantle it and pack all the parts in the cases . . .
But what about the whisky out of those cases! Tell me! Is it still ashore? . . .
Oh no!
No, no. It was night before you sailed. The cases were still on the quay, ready to be embarked. I took out all the bottles they contained, and put the pieces of my machine in their place . . .
Wretch! . . . Ignoramus! . . . Abominable Snowman! . . . I'll throw you overboard! Overboard, d'you hear? . . .

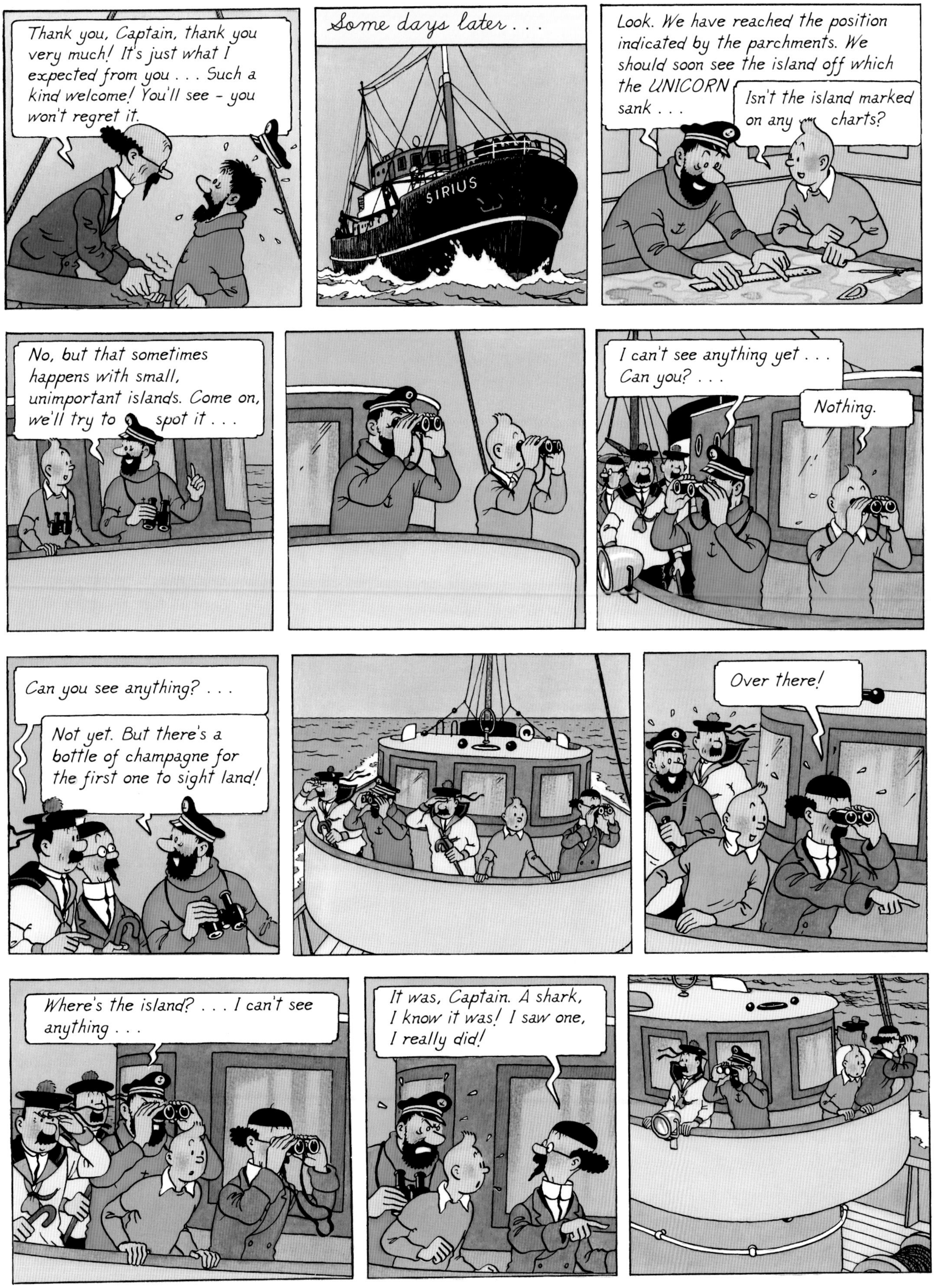
Thank you, Captain, thank you very much! It's just what I expected from you . . . Such a kind welcome! You'll see - you won't regret it.
Some days later . . .
SIRIUS
Look. We have reached the position indicated by the parchments. We should soon see the island off which the UNICORN sank . . .
Isn't the island marked on any charts?
No, but that sometimes happens with small, unimportant islands. Come on, we'll try to spot it . . .
I can't see anything yet . . . Can you? . . .
Nothing.
Can you see anything? . . .
Not yet. But there's a bottle of champagne for the first one to sight land!
Over there!
Where's the island? . . . I can't see anything . . .
It was, Captain. A shark, I know it was! I saw one, I really did!

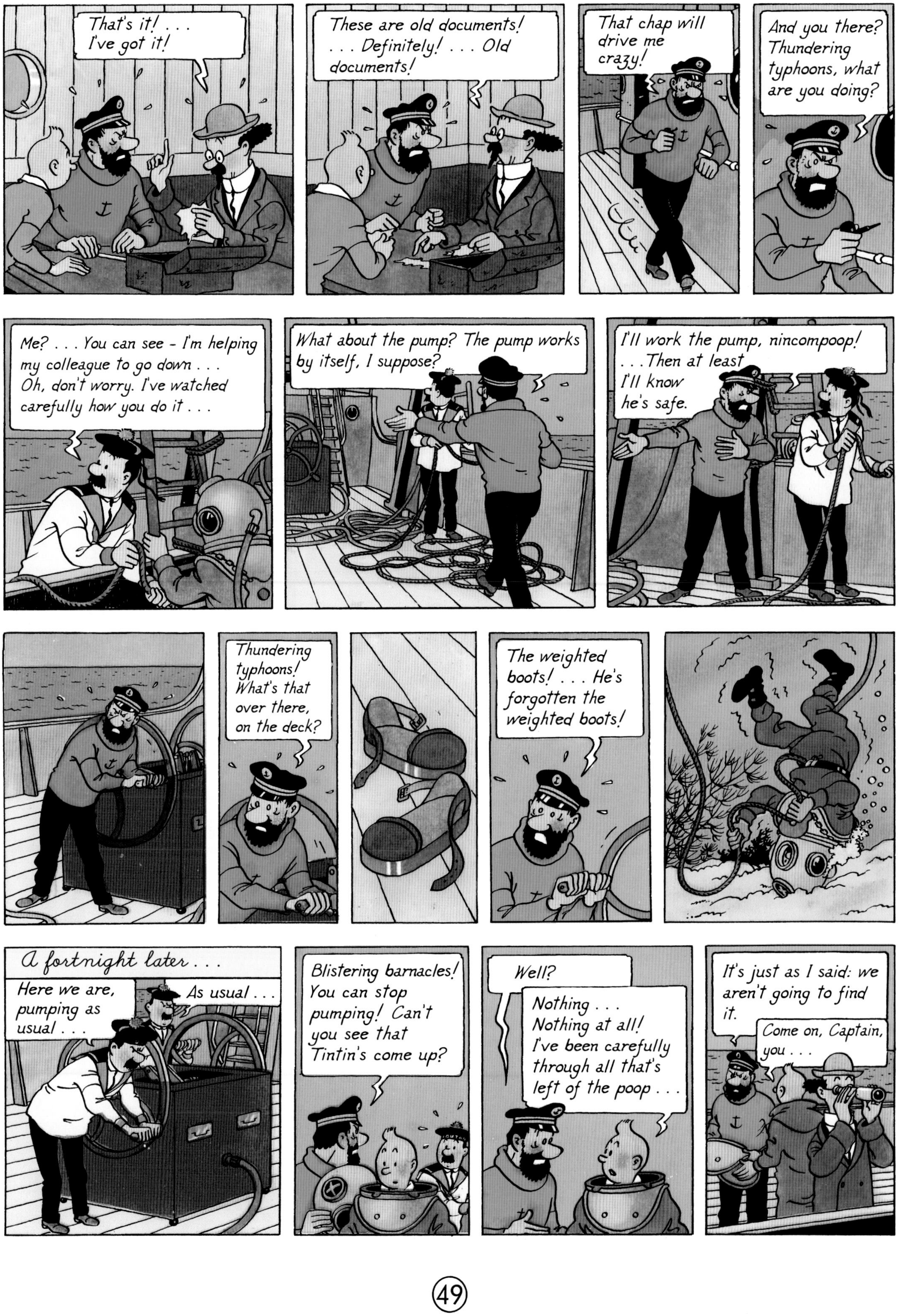

That's it! . . .
I've got it!
These are old documents! . . . Definitely! . . . Old documents!
That chap will drive me crazy!
And you there? Thundering typhoons, what are you doing?
Me? . . . You can see - I'm helping my colleague to go down . . . Oh, don't worry. I've watched carefully how you do it . . .
What about the pump? The pump works by itself, I suppose?
I'll work the pump, nincompoop! . . .Then at least I'll know he's safe.
Thundering typhoons! What's that over there, on the deck?
The weighted boots! . . . He's forgotten the weighted boots!
A fortnight later . . .
Here we are, pumping as usual . . .
As usual . . .
Blistering barnacles! You can stop pumping! Can't you see that Tintin's come up?
Well?
Nothing . . . Nothing at all! I've been carefully through all that's left of the poop . . .
It's just as I said: we aren't going to find it.
Come on, Captain, you . . .

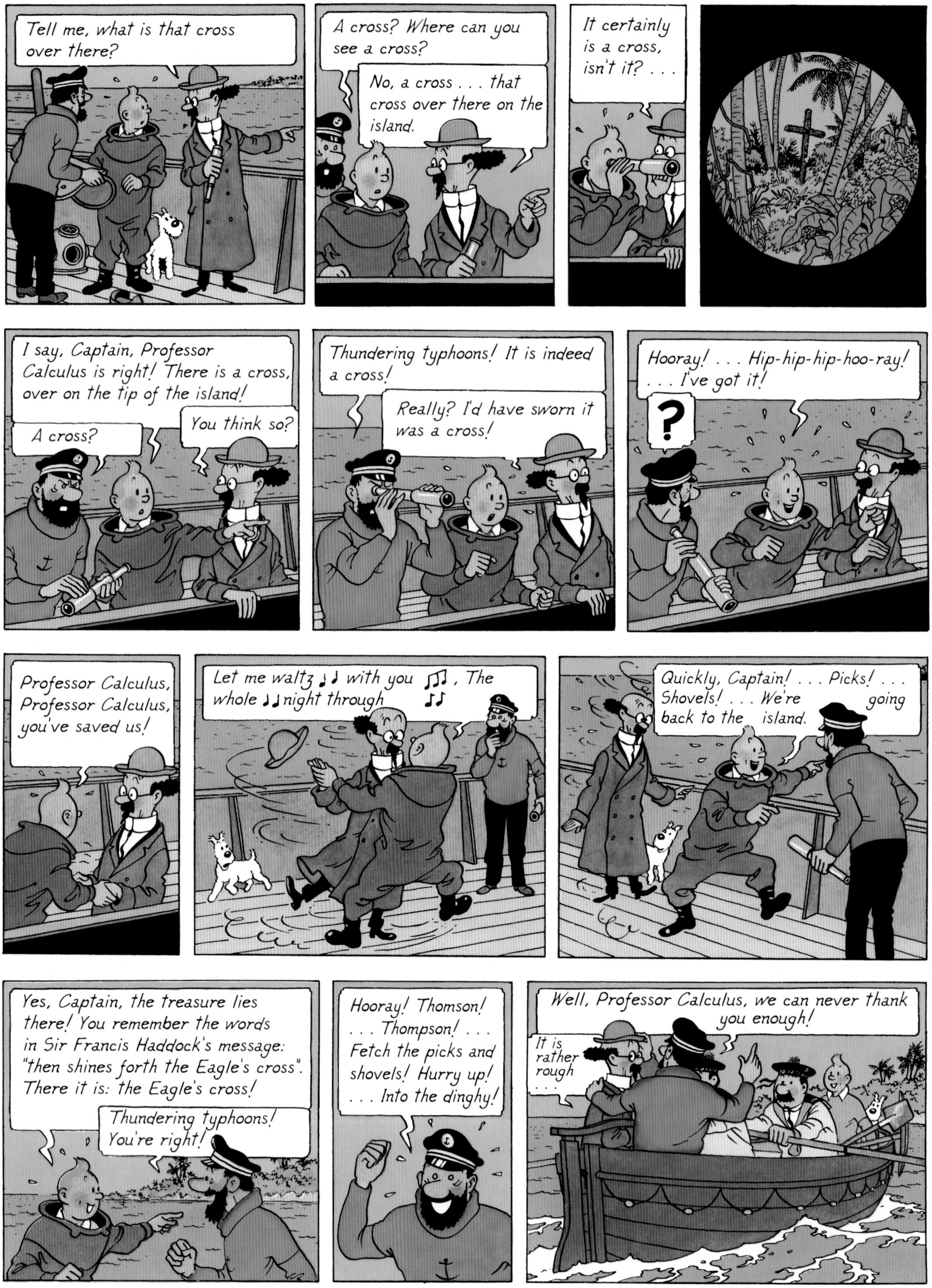

Tell me, what is that cross over there?
A cross? Where can you see a cross?
No, a cross . . . that cross over there on the island.
It certainly is a cross, isn't it? . . .
I say, Captain, Professor Calculus is right! There is a cross, over on the tip of the island!
A cross?
You think so?
Thundering typhoons! It is indeed a cross!
Really? I'd have sworn it was a cross!
Hooray! . . . Hip-hip-hip-hoo-ray! . . . I've got it!
?
Professor Calculus, Professor Calculus, you've saved us!
Let me waltz with you, The whole night through
Quickly, Captain! . . . Picks! . . . Shovels! . . . We're going back to the island.
Yes, Captain, the treasure lies there! You remember the words in Sir Francis Haddock's message: "then shines forth the Eagle's cross". There it is: the Eagle's cross!
Thundering typhoons! You're right!
Hooray! Thomson! . . . Thompson! . . . Fetch the picks and shovels! Hurry up! . . . Into the dinghy!
Well, Professor Calculus, we can never thank you enough!
It is rather rough . . .

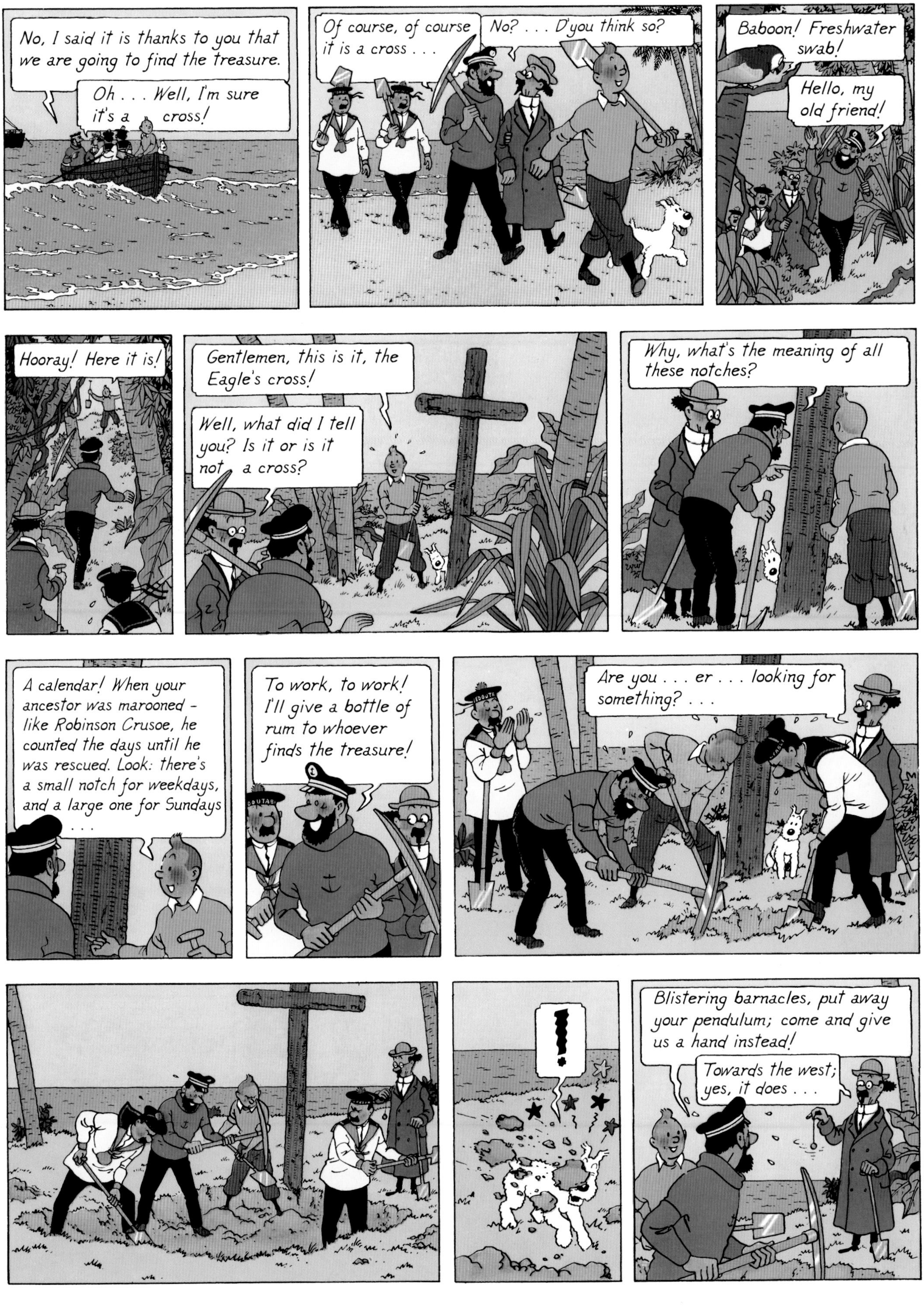
No, I said it is thanks to you that we are going to find the treasure.
Oh . . . Well, I'm sure it's a cross!
Of course, of course it is a cross . . .
No? . . . D'you think so?
Baboon! Freshwater swab!
Hello, my old friend!
Hooray! Here it is!
Gentlemen, this is it, the Eagle's cross!
Well, what did I tell you? Is it or is it not a cross?
Why, what's the meaning of all these notches?
A calendar! When your ancestor was marooned - like Robinson Crusoe, he counted the days until he was rescued. Look: there's a small notch for weekdays, and a large one for Sundays . . .
To work, to work! I'll give a bottle of rum to whoever finds the treasure!
Are you . . . er . . . looking for something? . . .
!
Blistering barnacles, put away your pendulum; come and give us a hand instead!
Towards the west; yes, it does . . .

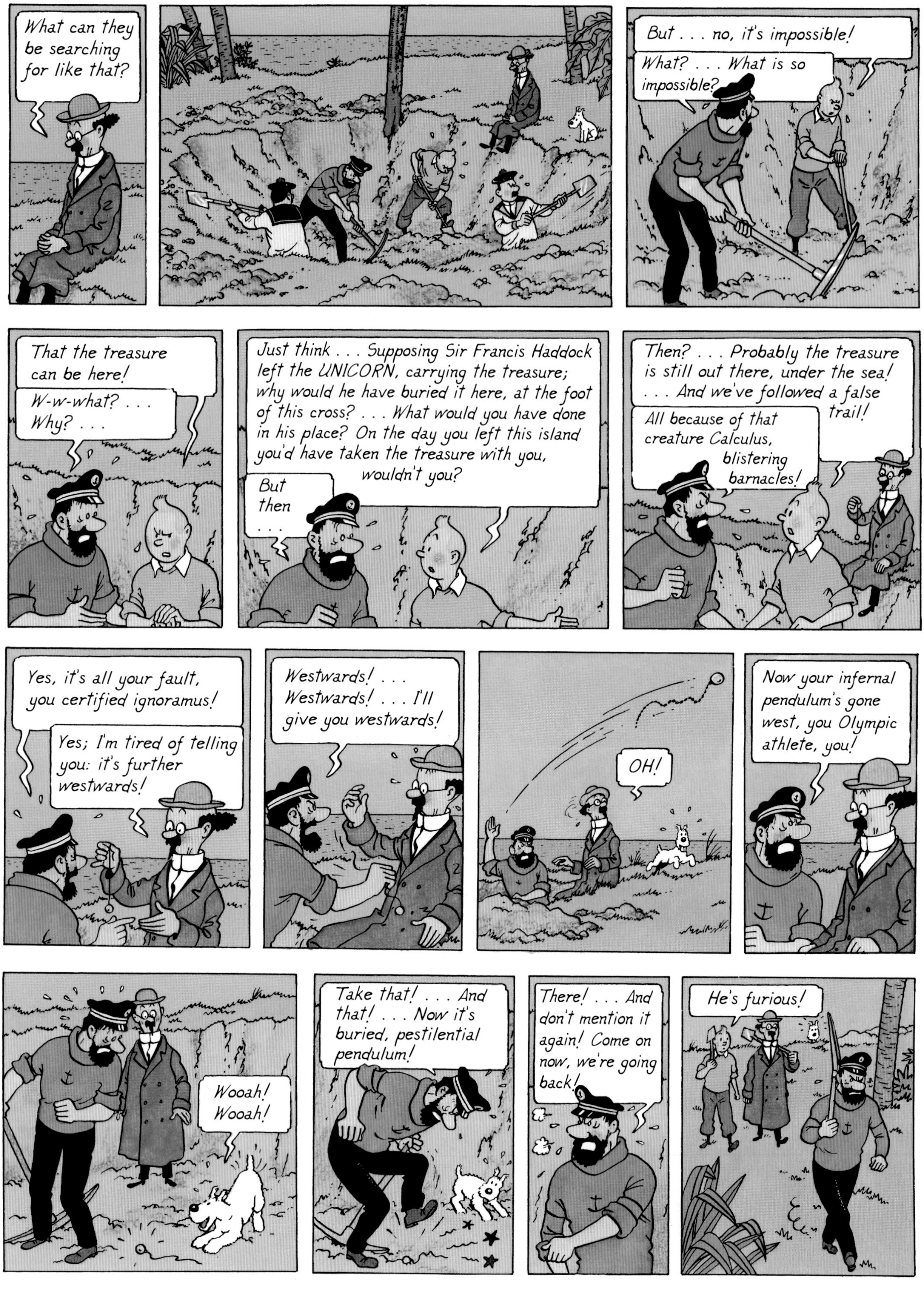
What can they be searching for like that?
But . . . no, it's impossible!
What? . . . What is so impossible?
That the treasure can be here!
W-w-what? . . . Why? . . .
Just think . . . Supposing Sir Francis Haddock left the UNICORN, carrying the treasure; why would he have buried it here, at the foot of this cross? . . . What would you have done in his place? On the day you left this island you'd have taken the treasure with you, wouldn't you?
But then . . .
Then? . . . Probably the treasure is still out there, under the sea! . . . And we've followed a false trail!
All because of that creature Calculus, blistering barnacles!
Yes, it's all your fault, you certified ignoramus!
Yes; I'm tired of telling you: it's further westwards!
Westwards! . . . Westwards! . . . I'll give you westwards!
OH!
Now your infernal pendulum's gone west, you Olympic athlete, you!
Wooah! Wooah!
Take that! . . . And that! . . . Now it's buried, pestilential pendulum!
There! . . . And don't mention it again! Come on now, we're going back!
He's furious!

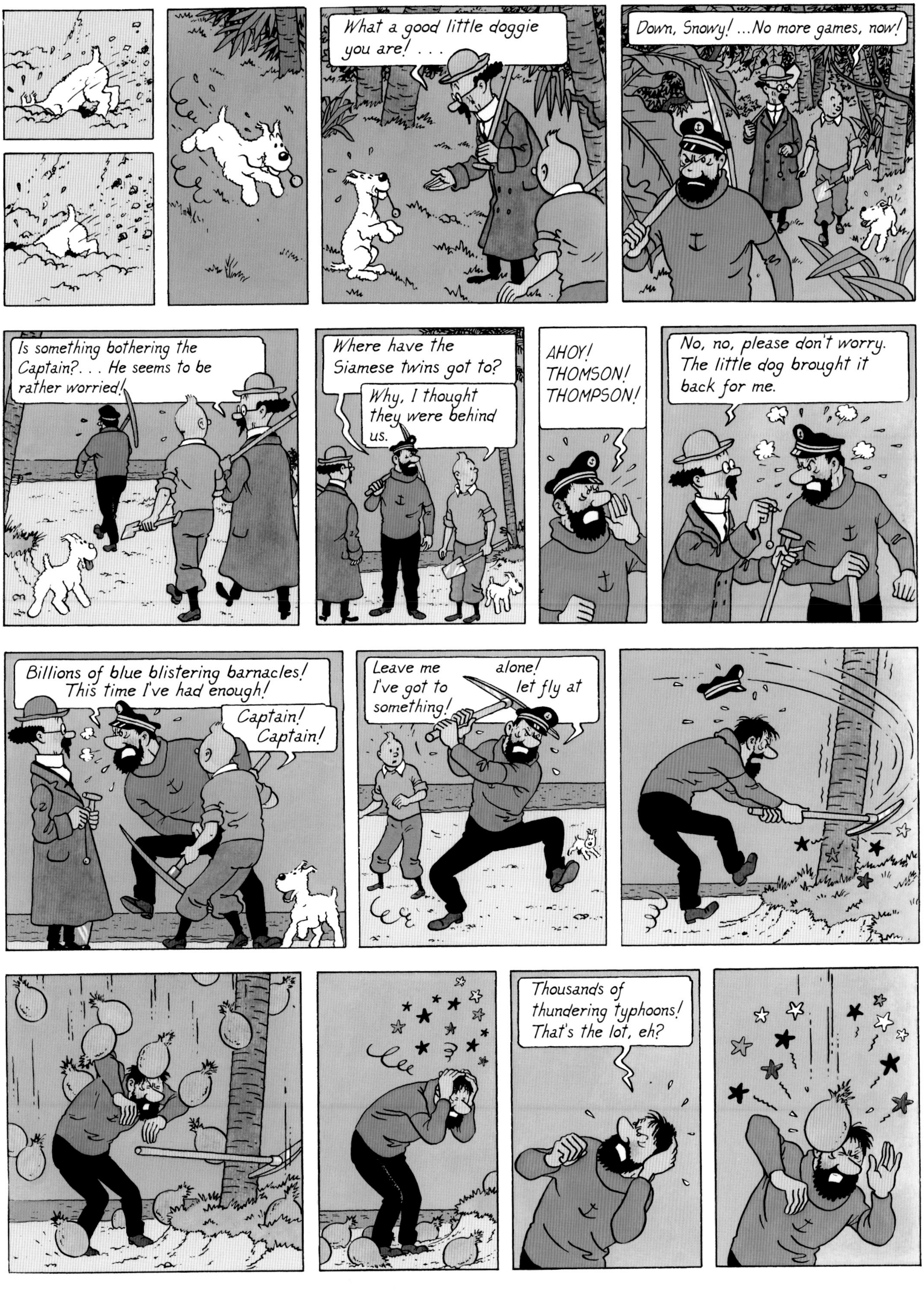

What a good little doggie you are! . . .
Down, Snowy! ...No more games, now!
Is something bothering the Captain?. . . He seems to be rather worried!
Where have the Siamese twins got to?
Why, I thought they were behind us.
AHOY! THOMSON! THOMPSON!
No, no, please don't worry. The little dog brought it back for me.
Billions of blue blistering barnacles! This time I've had enough!
Captain! Captain!
Leave me alone! I've got to let fly at something!
Thousands of thundering typhoons! That's the lot, eh?

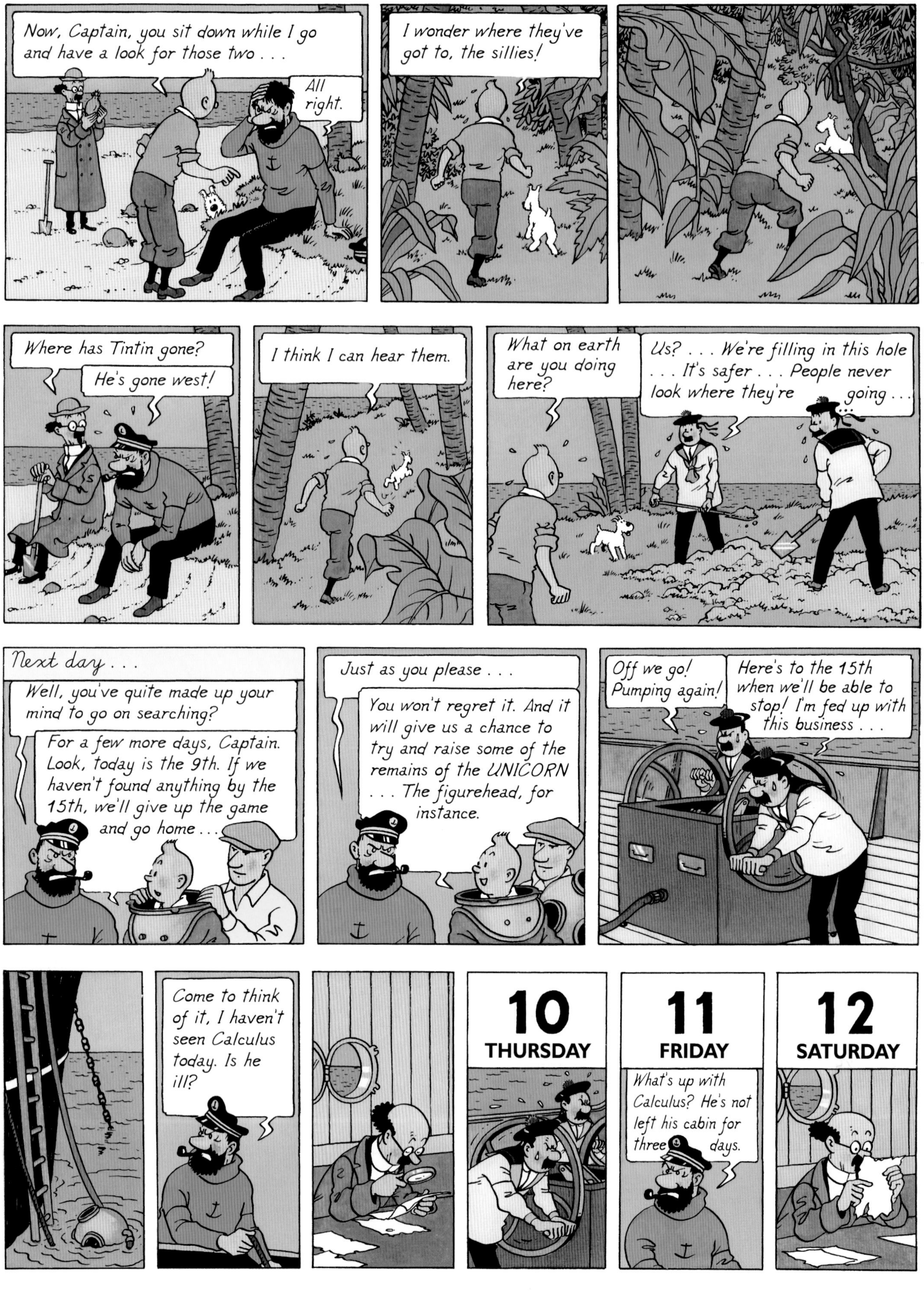
Now, Captain, you sit down while I go and have a look for those two . . .
All right.
I wonder where they've got to, the sillies!
Where has Tintin gone?
He's gone west!
I think I can hear them.
What on earth are you doing here?
Us? . . . We're filling in this hole . . . It's safer . . . People never look where they're going . . .
Next day . . .
Well, you've quite made up your mind to go on searching?
For a few more days, Captain. Look, today is the 9th. If we haven't found anything by the 15th, we'll give up the game and go home . . .
Just as you please . . .
You won't regret it. And it will give us a chance to try and raise some of the remains of the UNICORN . . . The figurehead, for instance.
Off we go! Pumping again!
Here's to the 15th when we'll be able to stop! I'm fed up with this business . . .
Come to think of it, I haven't seen Calculus today. Is he ill?
10 THURSDAY
11 FRIDAY
What's up with Calculus? He's not left his cabin for three days.
12 SATURDAY

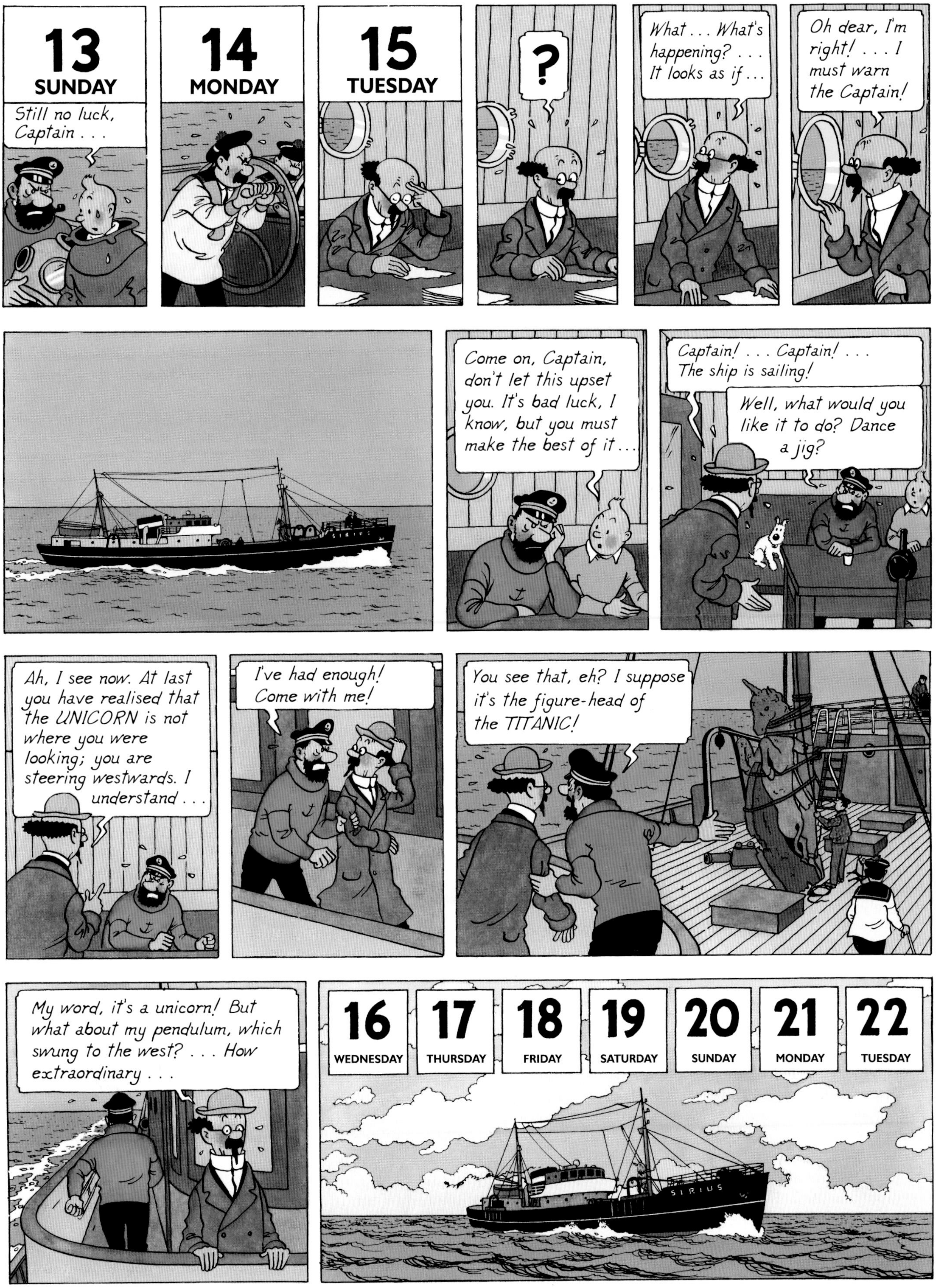

13
SUNDAY
14
MONDAY
15
TUESDAY
Still no luck, Captain . . .
?
What . . . What's happening? . . . It looks as if . . .
Oh dear, I'm right! . . . I must warn the Captain!
SIRIUS
Come on, Captain, don't let this upset you. It's bad luck, I know, but you must make the best of it . . .
Captain! . . . Captain! . . . The ship is sailing!
Well, what would you like it to do? Dance a jig?
Ah, I see now. At last you have realised that the UNICORN is not where you were looking; you are steering westwards. I understand . . .
I've had enough! Come with me!
You see that, eh? I suppose it's the figure-head of the TITANIC!
My word, it's a unicorn! But what about my pendulum, which swung to the west? . . . How extraordinary . . .
16
WEDNESDAY
17
THURSDAY
18
FRIDAY
19
SATURDAY
20
SUNDAY
21
MONDAY
22
TUESDAY
SIRIUS

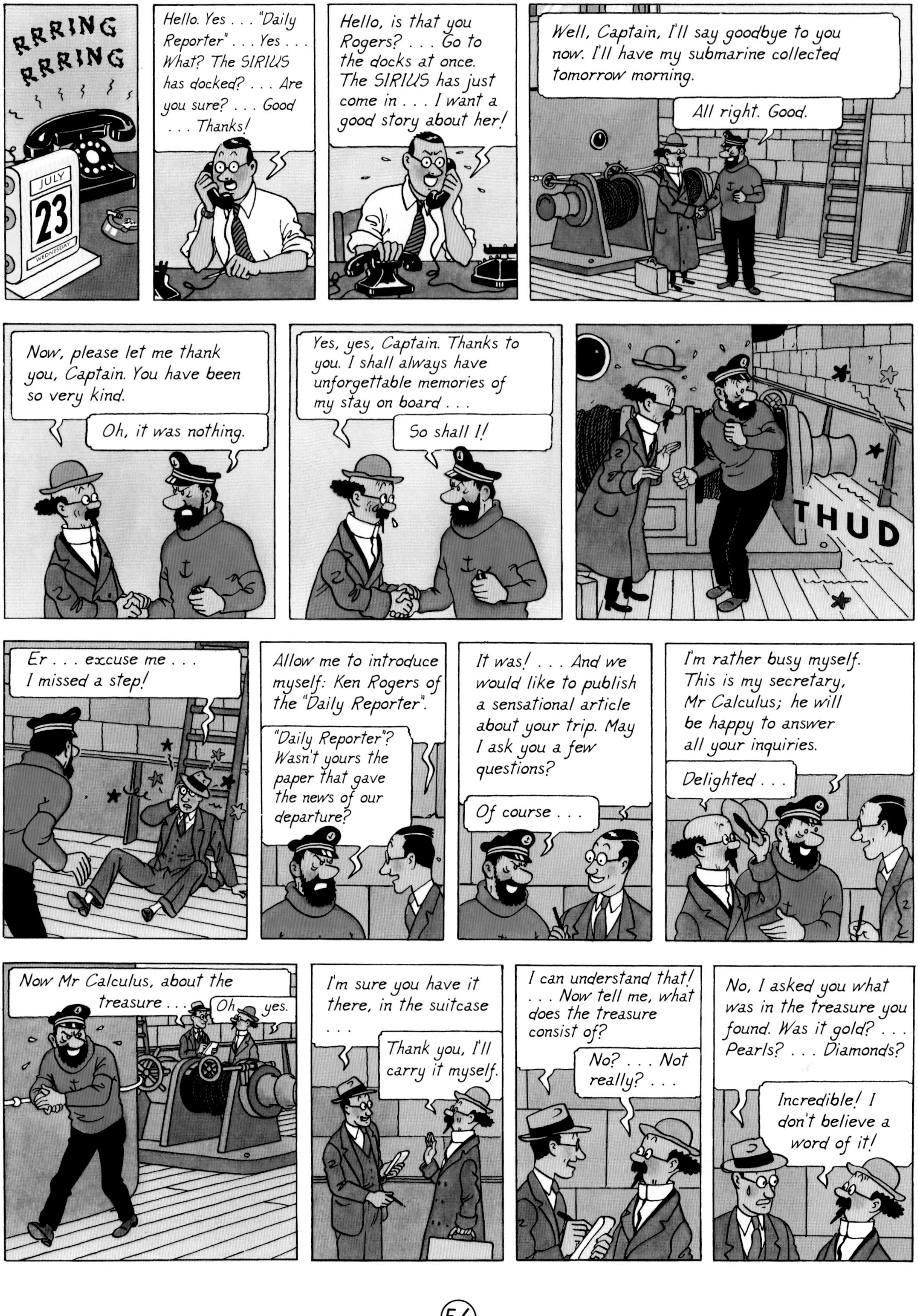
RRRING RRRING
JULY
23
WEDNESDAY
Hello. Yes . . . "Daily Reporter" . . . Yes . . . What? The SIRIUS has docked? . . . Are you sure? . . . Good . . . Thanks!
Hello, is that you Rogers? . . . Go to the docks at once. The SIRIUS has just come in . . . I want a good story about her!
Well, Captain, I'll say goodbye to you now. I'll have my submarine collected tomorrow morning.
All right. Good.
Now, please let me thank you, Captain. You have been so very kind.
Oh, it was nothing.
Yes, yes, Captain. Thanks to you. I shall always have unforgettable memories of my stay on board . . .
So shall I!
THUD
Er . . . excuse me . . . I missed a step!
Allow me to introduce myself: Ken Rogers of the "Daily Reporter".
"Daily Reporter"? Wasn't yours the paper that gave the news of our departure?
It was! . . . And we would like to publish a sensational article about your trip. May I ask you a few questions?
Of course . . .
I'm rather busy myself. This is my secretary, Mr Calculus; he will be happy to answer all your inquiries.
Delighted . . .
Now Mr Calculus, about the treasure . . .
Oh yes.
I'm sure you have it there, in the suitcase . . .
Thank you, I'll carry it myself.
I can understand that! . . . Now tell me, what does the treasure consist of?
No? . . . Not really? . . .
No, I asked you what was in the treasure you found. Was it gold? . . . Pearls? . . . Diamonds?
Incredible! I don't believe a word of it!

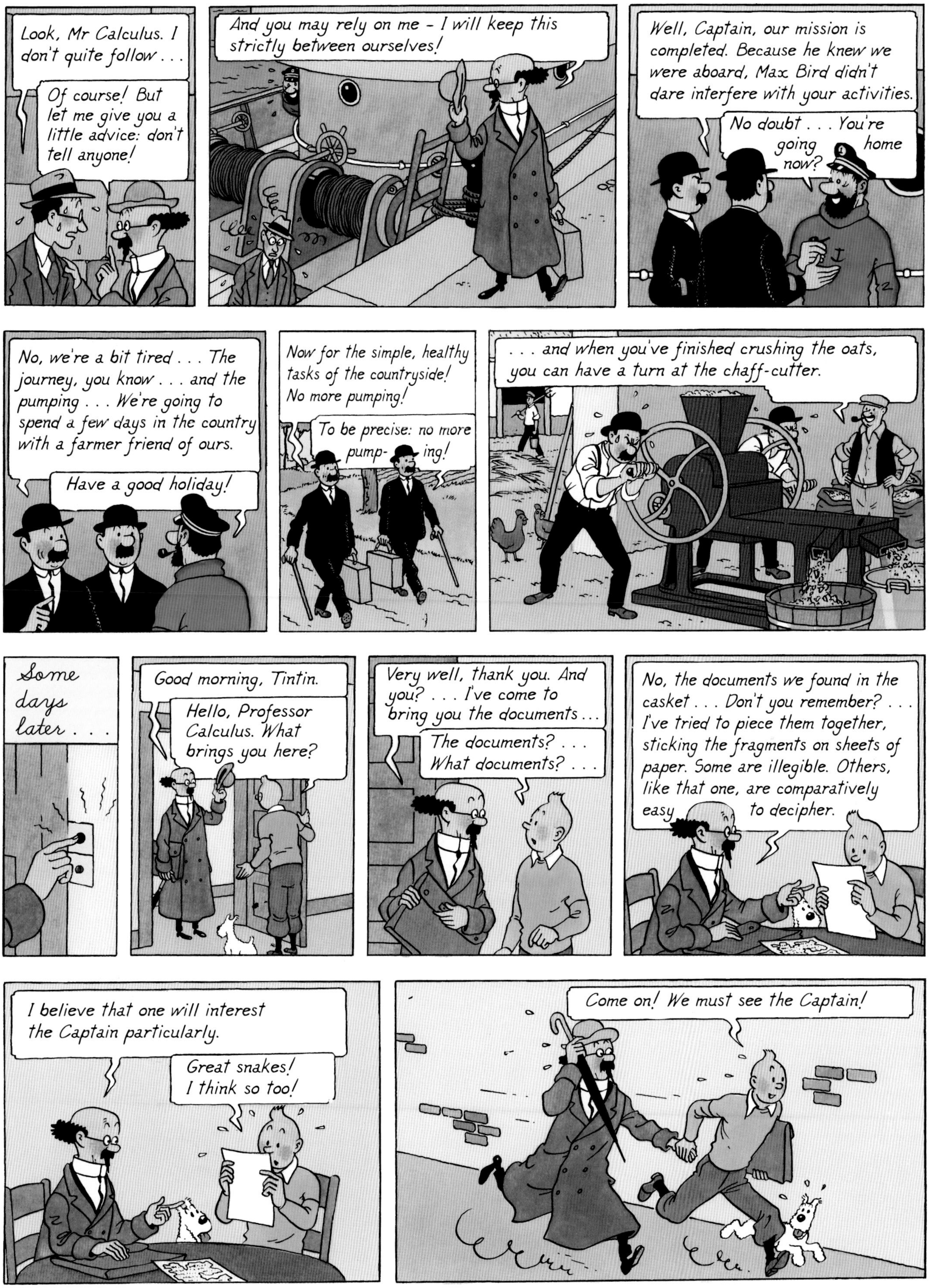

Look, Mr Calculus. I don't quite follow . . .
Of course! But let me give you a little advice: don't tell anyone!
And you may rely on me - I will keep this strictly between ourselves!
Well, Captain, our mission is completed. Because he knew we were aboard, Max Bird didn't dare interfere with your activities.
No doubt . . . You're going home now?
No, we're a bit tired . . . The journey, you know . . . and the pumping . . . We're going to spend a few days in the country with a farmer friend of ours.
Have a good holiday!
Now for the simple, healthy tasks of the countryside! No more pumping!
To be precise: no more pump- ing!
. . . and when you've finished crushing the oats, you can have a turn at the chaff-cutter.
Some days later . . .
Good morning, Tintin.
Hello, Professor Calculus. What brings you here?
Very well, thank you. And you? . . . I've come to bring you the documents . . .
The documents? . . . What documents? . . .
No, the documents we found in the casket . . . Don't you remember? . . . I've tried to piece them together, sticking the fragments on sheets of paper. Some are illegible. Others, like that one, are comparatively easy to decipher.
I believe that one will interest the Captain particularly.
Great snakes! I think so too!
Come on! We must see the Captain!

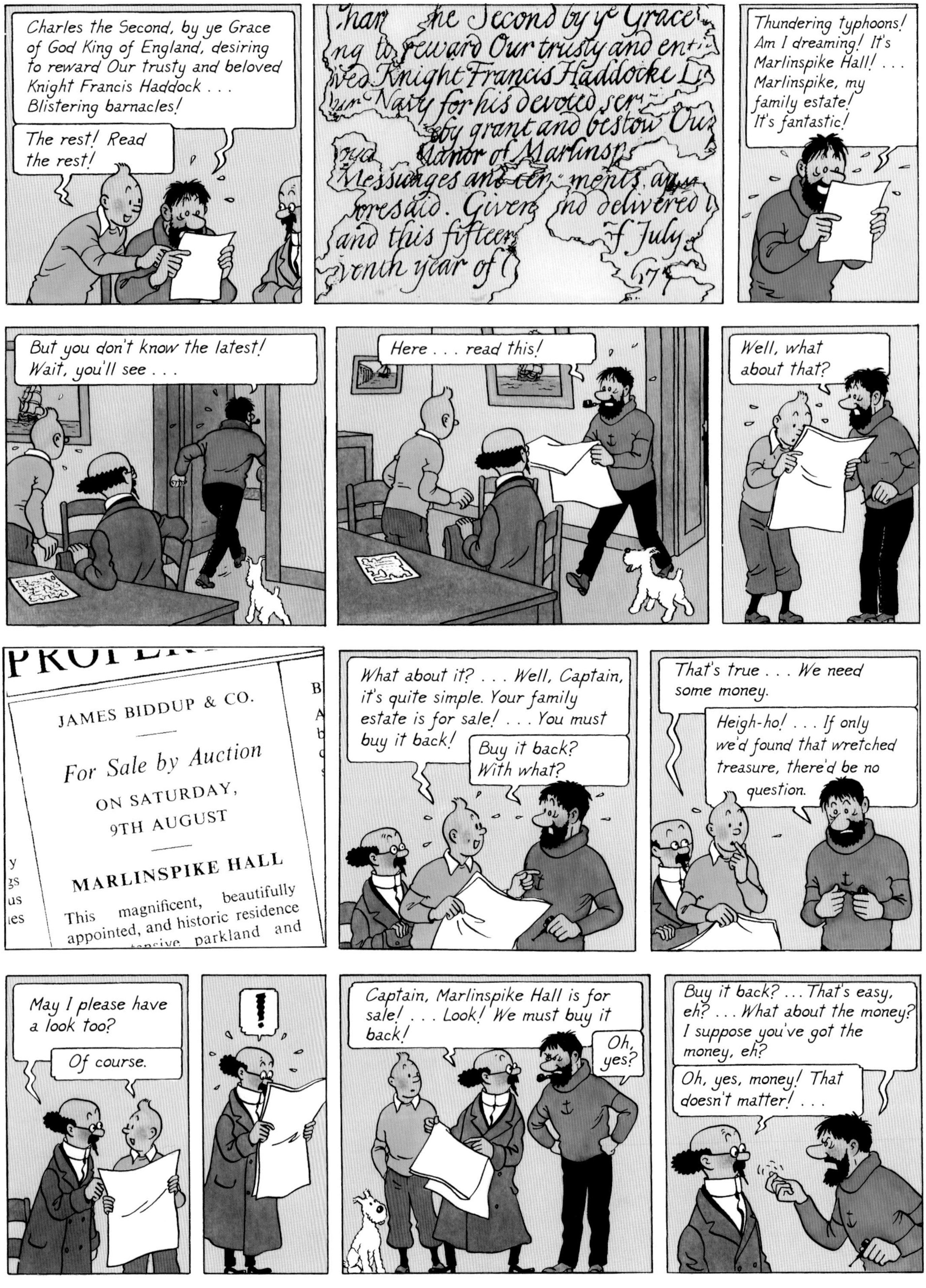
Charles the Second, by ye Grace of God King of England, desiring to reward Our trusty and beloved Knight Francis Haddock . . . Blistering barnacles!
The rest! Read the rest!
he Second by ye Grace
ng to reward Our trusty and en
ved Knight Francis Haddocke
Navy for his devoted ser
by grant and bestow Our
Manor of Marlinsp
Messuages and ten ments, a
resaid. Given and delivered
and this fifteen f July
venth year of
Thundering typhoons! Am I dreaming! It's Marlinspike Hall! . . . Marlinspike, my family estate! It's fantastic!
But you don't know the latest! Wait, you'll see . . .
Here . . . read this!
Well, what about that?
JAMES BIDDUP & CO.
For Sale by Auction
ON SATURDAY, 9TH AUGUST
MARLINSPIKE HALL
This magnificent, beautifully appointed, and historic residence
parkland and
What about it? . . . Well, Captain, it's quite simple. Your family estate is for sale! . . . You must buy it back!
Buy it back? With what?
That's true . . . We need some money.
Heigh-ho! . . . If only we'd found that wretched treasure, there'd be no question.
May I please have a look too?
Of course.
!
Captain, Marlinspike Hall is for sale! . . . Look! We must buy it back!
Oh, yes?
Buy it back? . . . That's easy, eh? . . . What about the money? I suppose you've got the money, eh?
Oh, yes, money! That doesn't matter! . . .

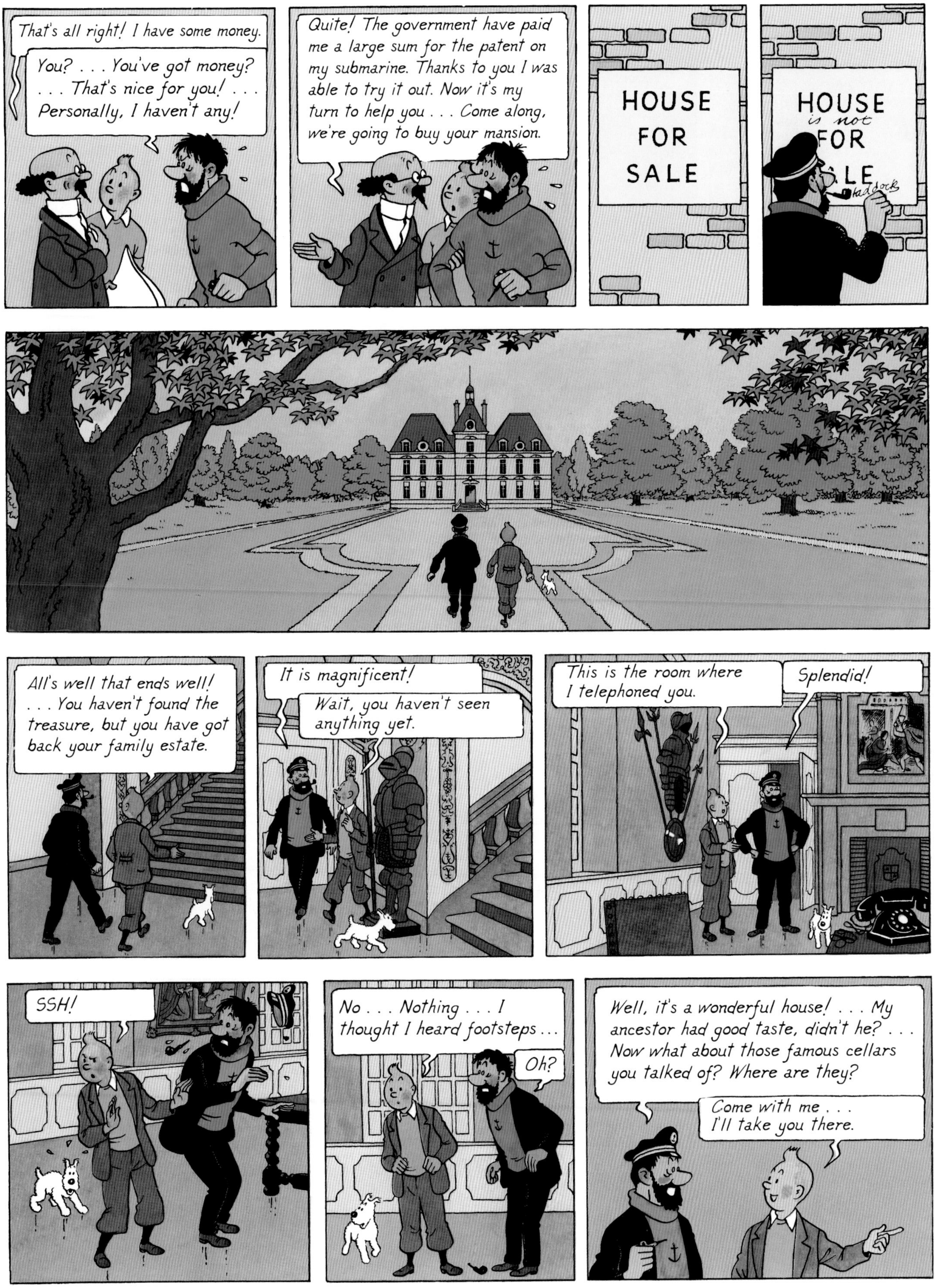
That's all right! I have some money.
You? . . . You've got money? . . . That's nice for you! . . . Personally, I haven't any!
Quite! The government have paid me a large sum for the patent on my submarine. Thanks to you I was able to try it out. Now it's my turn to help you . . . Come along, we're going to buy your mansion.
HOUSE FOR SALE
HOUSE is not FOR
Haddock
All's well that ends well! . . . You haven't found the treasure, but you have got back your family estate.
It is magnificent!
Wait, you haven't seen anything yet.
This is the room where I telephoned you.
Splendid!
SSH!
No . . . Nothing . . . I thought I heard footsteps . . .
Oh?
Well, it's a wonderful house! . . . My ancestor had good taste, didn't he? . . . Now what about those famous cellars you talked of? Where are they?
Come with me . . . I'll take you there.

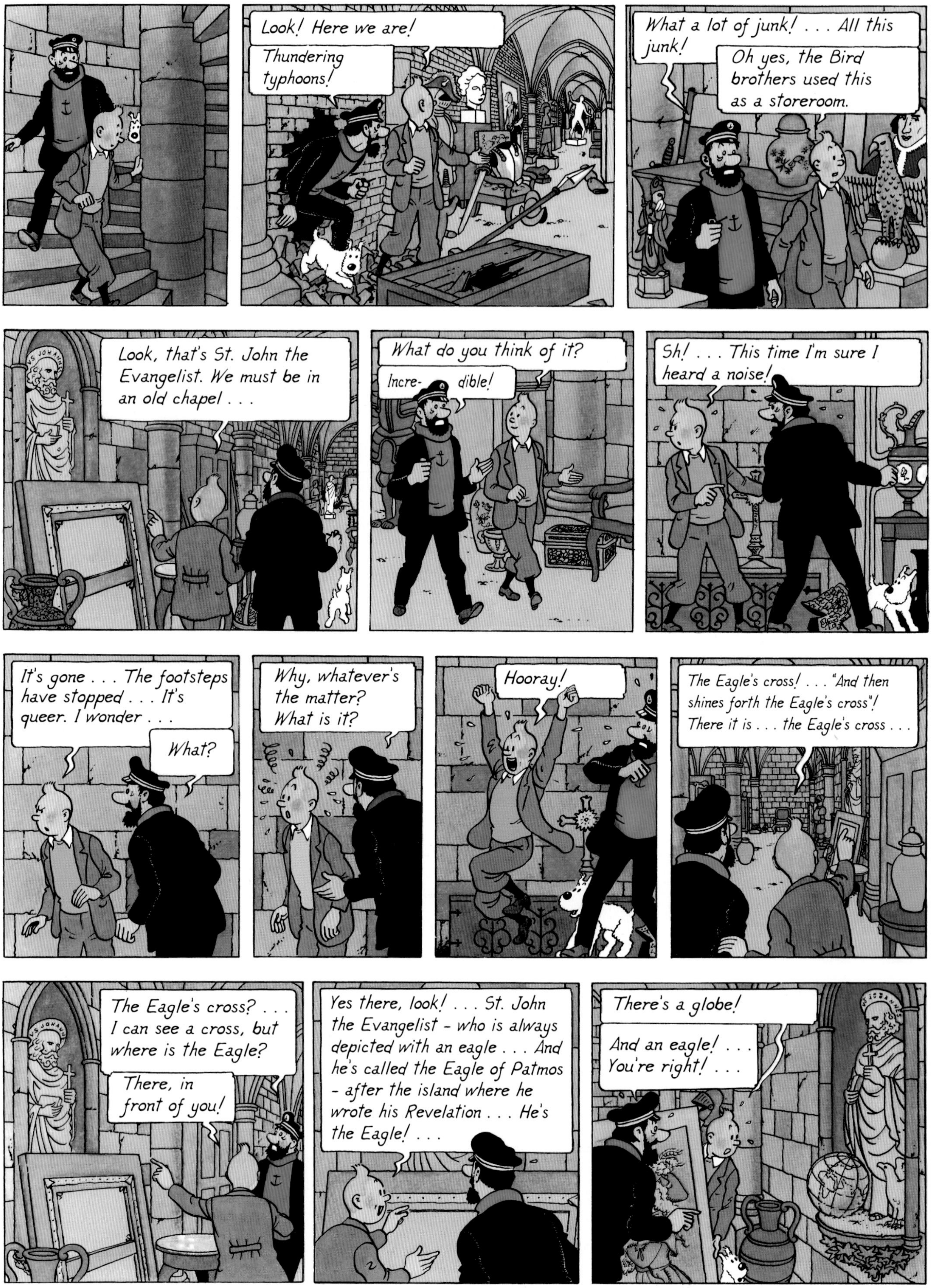
Look! Here we are!
Thundering typhoons!
What a lot of junk! . . . All this junk!
Oh yes, the Bird brothers used this as a storeroom.
Look, that's St. John the Evangelist. We must be in an old chapel . . .
What do you think of it?
Incre- dible!
Sh! . . . This time I'm sure I heard a noise!
It's gone . . . The footsteps have stopped . . . It's queer. I wonder . . .
What?
Why, whatever's the matter? What is it?
Hooray!
The Eagle's cross! . . . "And then shines forth the Eagle's cross"! There it is . . . the Eagle's cross . . .
The Eagle's cross? . . . I can see a cross, but where is the Eagle?
There, in front of you!
Yes there, look! . . . St. John the Evangelist - who is always depicted with an eagle . . . And he's called the Eagle of Patmos - after the island where he wrote his Revelation . . . He's the Eagle! . . .
There's a globe!
And an eagle! . . . You're right! . . .

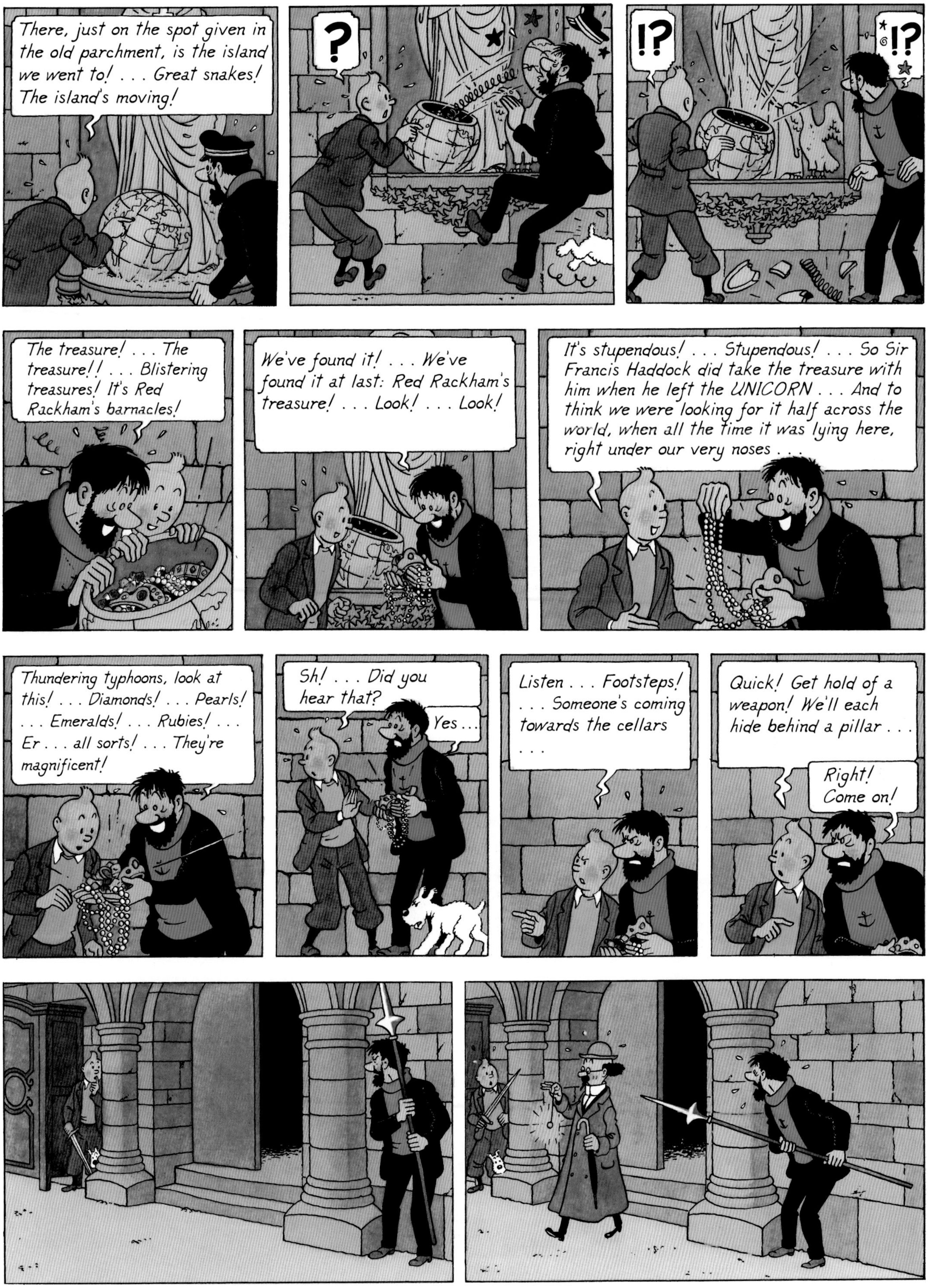
There, just on the spot given in the old parchment, is the island we went to! . . . Great snakes! The island's moving!
?
!?
!?
The treasure! . . . The treasure!! . . . Blistering treasures! It's Red Rackham's barnacles!
We've found it! . . . We've found it at last: Red Rackham's treasure! . . . Look! . . . Look!
It's stupendous! . . . Stupendous! . . . So Sir Francis Haddock did take the treasure with him when he left the UNICORN . . . And to think we were looking for it half across the world, when all the time it was lying here, right under our very noses . . .
Thundering typhoons, look at this! . . . Diamonds! . . . Pearls! . . . Emeralds! . . . Rubies! . . . Er . . . all sorts! . . . They're magnificent!
Sh! . . . Did you hear that?
Yes . . .
Listen . . . Footsteps! . . . Someone's coming towards the cellars . . .
Quick! Get hold of a weapon! We'll each hide behind a pillar . . .
Right! Come on!

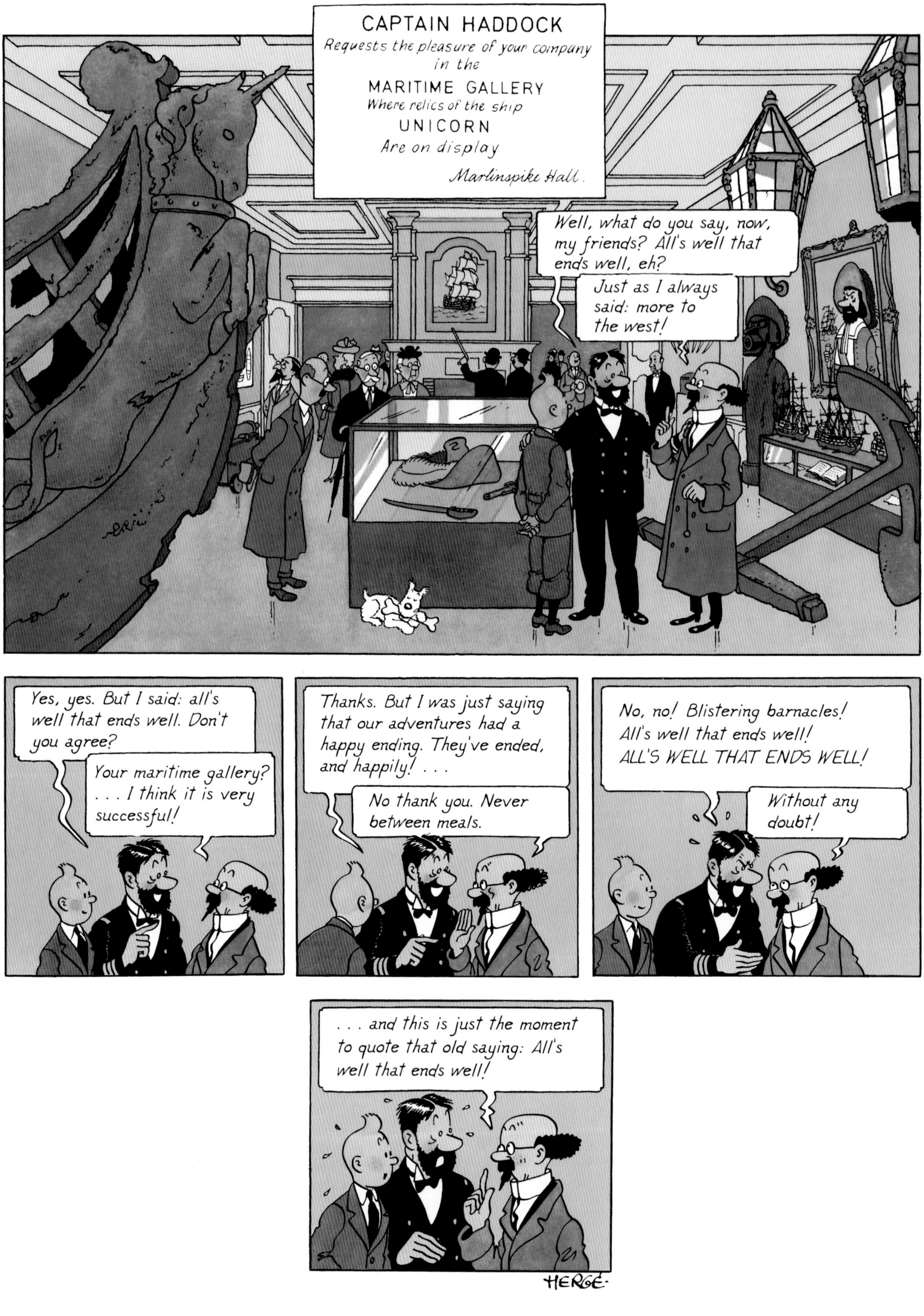
CAPTAIN HADDOCK
Requests the pleasure of your company
in the
MARITIME GALLERY
Where relics of the ship
UNICORN
Are on display
Marlinspike Hall.
Well, what do you say, now, my friends? All's well that ends well, eh?
Just as I always said: more to the west!
Yes, yes. But I said: all's well that ends well. Don't you agree?
Your maritime gallery? . . . I think it is very successful!
Thanks. But I was just saying that our adventures had a happy ending. They've ended, and happily! . . .
No thank you. Never between meals.
No, no! Blistering barnacles! All's well that ends well! ALL'S WELL THAT ENDS WELL!
Without any doubt!
. . . and this is just the moment to quote that old saying: All's well that ends well!
HERGÉ